A Connoisseur's Case

Michael Innes

Penguin Books

Penguin Books Ltd, Harmondsworth, Middlesex, England
Penguin Books Pty Ltd, Ringwood, Victoria, Australia

First published by Victor Gollancz 1962
Published in Penguin Books 1966
Copyright © J. I. M. Stewart, 1962

Made and printed in Great Britain by
Cox & Wyman Ltd, London, Reading and Fakenham
Set in Monotype Baskerville

Penguin Book c2410

A Connoisseur's Case

Michael Innes is the pseudonym of J. I. M. Stewart,
who has been a Student of Christ Church, Oxford,
since 1949. He was born in 1906 and was educated
at Edinburgh Academy and Oriel College,
Oxford. He was lecturer in English at the University
of Leeds from 1930 to 1935, and spent the succeeding
ten years as Jury Professor of English in the
University of Adelaide, South Australia.

He has published five novels and a volume of
short stories, as well as many detective stories and
broadcast scripts under the pseudonym of Michael
Innes. His *Eight Modern Writers* appeared in 1963
as the final volume of *The Oxford History of English
Literature*. Michael Innes is married and has five
children.

Chapter One

'And that,' Judith Appleby said, 'must be Scroop House.' She took her finger from the map and pointed across the valley. 'Get out the guide-book, John.'

Obediently, John Appleby unhitched his rucksack and rummaged in it.

'Here you are,' he said. 'But I don't expect it's on view.' He didn't entirely share his wife's fondness for perambulating the stately homes of England. One – he had long ago decided – was not all that different from another.

'William Chambers,' Judith said. She had expertly flicked over the pages. 'Finished in 1786.'

'Late,' Appleby said disparagingly. 'Practically Victorian.'

'Don't be idiotic.' Judith had climbed a gate and was perched on it. 'It may have heavenly *chinoiseries*.'

'Most improbable.' Appleby spoke briskly. If he had rather less than Judith's enthusiasm, he had rather more than her grasp of relevant facts. 'Chambers, you know, really went to China when he was a young man. His Chinese temples and furniture and so on are, in consequence, almost authentic. They have all the tasteless and gimcrack quality of the real thing with nothing of the more engaging fantasy that more ignorant designers brought to it. Think of Edwards and Darly. Garden chairs made of roots, and that kind of thing. Most attractive. But Chambers – no. Let's get on.' He held out his hand hopefully for the guide-book. 'We might get across the valley before eating those sandwiches, don't you think?'

But Judith, of course, was not to be bullied. She read on.

'Bother!' she said presently. 'It doesn't say who lives there. Stupid of it.'

'My dear Judith, what good could it possibly do you to know who owns Scroop House? It would be out of your head again by breakfast-time tomorrow.'

'You're right that the place isn't on public view.'

'Then there you are.'

'Exactly.' Judith jumped down from the gate. 'If we knew his name, we could ask for him.'

Appleby, who was fond of admitting that he was a very conventional man, stared at his wife aghast.

'Ask for him? We can't barge in on a total stranger.'

'He can't be a total stranger to Uncle Julius. Uncle Julius knows all the other nobs in the county, I suppose. We could explain I was his niece.'

Appleby's alarm grew. This social outrage was already vivid in his imagination.

'It just isn't done,' he said.

'Then, of course, we can't do it.' Judith had picked up her walking-stick and was moving briskly forward. She found her husband's attitude highly entertaining. In his time John had, after all, done quite a number of things that are not commonly done. When they got inside Scroop House – as they were certainly going to do – he would cheer up and look civilly around him.

'In the eighteenth century,' she said, 'it was hardly polite for a traveller to ignore a gentleman's seat. You drove up, announced yourself, and an upper servant showed you round. If the owner was feeling sociable, he would appear and receive you.'

'And Madeira and cake would then be served in the library.' Appleby was resigned. 'Let's hope for that, too. Perhaps we can bring out our sandwiches and eat them at the same time. The upper servant will clear away the crumbs.'

'Of course we won't try if you don't want to.' Judith now said this as a matter of form. 'I expect Uncle Julius would drive us over and introduce us tomorrow. Only his gout does seem to be rather bad, and he is very preoccupied with the atlas. He likes having us down, but he likes us going off like this for the day.'

'Quite so.' Appleby was aware that Colonel Julius Raven's *Atlas and Entomology of the Dry-Fly Streams of England with an Appendix on Northern Britain* was to be a work of the first order of importance. Being an intermittent angler himself, he had even contributed some notes, and this had raised him greatly in the old gentleman's regard. 'Whether your uncle is familiarly acquainted with the chap at Scroop House,' Appleby went on, 'will depend entirely on the quality of the chap's water.'

'Or earlier history as a fisherman. Uncle Julius would go any distance to talk about Indian carp. He has a story to tell about playing a sixty pound *mahseer*. Not that he hasn't other interests as well. He likes hearing you talk about Scotland Yard. All those extraordinary crimes and horrors. He says you never tell him of a second-rate one – that you have a connoisseur's attitude to your job.'

'Dear me.' Appleby sounded not particularly gratified by this description.

'And it makes a change for the old man. Those sort of things don't happen down here.'

Appleby's glance travelled over the quiet valley.

'No,' he said. 'I don't suppose they do – praise the Lord.'

They walked on, and Scroop House disappeared among trees. But even at a distance it had declared itself as a tolerably imposing pile: the sort of place one feels one must have heard of at one time or another. Not that its exterior was showy; it pretended to be nothing more than a place to live in – but to live in in a pretty large if reticent way. The centre was perhaps a double cube, and another cube, one storey lower, had been bisected and placed at each end. Beyond these again were two compact wings, and the low-pitched roofs of these provided the only diagonals admitted in the entire rectangular composition. Even the portico – which one could guess to be Tuscan Doric – had the same flat lines as the main parapet above. Apart from four sparsely placed urns, the building ended off as bleakly as a biscuit tin. This was what the Applebys had glimpsed, framed between enormous beech trees and with a beech copse on its eastern flank. In front, a well timbered park sloped down to the bottom of the shallow valley.

'Have we to get across a stream?' Appleby asked.

Judith glanced at the map as she walked, and shook her head.

'Only the old canal. It's disused now, but there's still water in it. This stretch of it runs pretty well due east and west.'

'But that doesn't make sense.' Appleby was studying the contours of the land. 'The valley's closed to the west by those quite sizeable hills.'

'It goes through a tunnel that's nearly three miles long. We ought to see that too. The book calls it one of the major engineering performances of the entire English canal system. And it seems that it was all rather a flop. Partly because the railways came along in the disastrous way they did. And partly because, on the highest stretch of the canal to the east, they hadn't been too hot on their geology. It wouldn't hold water.'

'Disadvantageous,' Appleby said. 'But we're still quite high up here.'

'Yes. Beyond the tunnel, it seems, the canal drops through a long series of locks to the estuary. That must have cost money too.'

'I expect the fellow who got Chambers to run up Scroop House for him had a hand in making the canal as well. There was often local money in these affairs. And it sounds as if he must have dropped some. Perhaps that's why the house looks a bit bleak.'

Judith shook her head.

'They're often like that at that period. Ashlar faced with plaster, and with just a few architectural features in dressed stone. They put their money into really lavish decoration of the interior. It was all part of the social set-up. Outsiders didn't get much change from you. But you did your fellow insiders proud.' Judith paused to climb a stile. 'And that' – she added, not very logically – 'is why we're going to be insiders ourselves.'

'I think that we ought at least to see the tunnel first. It will provide something to talk about over the cake and Madeira.'

'Very well.' Judith had seized upon this false move instantly. 'There's a pub at this end of it, so we can get a drink with our lunch. And here's the canal.' She glanced at the map again. 'The pub's about two miles on. We follow the towpath.'

This wasn't too easy. The path was much overgrown with bramble and brier; there were places in which it had almost crumbled away; and recent rain had made it slippery underfoot.

'Country-folk,' Appleby said, 'seem to be following towns-people in giving up the use of their legs. Here's a perfectly good straight route from somewhere to somewhere else, but it's as completely unused as the canal is.'

Judith dropped on her hands and knees in order to crawl under a small thicket of blackthorn.

'Any sort of wayfaring is out,' she said. 'Take going to school. Parents who could remember perfectly well, if they

9

tried, that walking there and back was the nicest part of the day, now feel that their children are being cheated of something if the local authority doesn't send round a bus. The kids are treated as if they were chronic invalids.'

'But we are elderly folk, you know. Our attitude to these things is nostalgic and sentimental. Children straying down the lanes, trailing their satchels and splashing through the puddles and keeping an informed eye open for birds' nests, make a very pretty picture. But probably the young people themselves now prefer the bus. And what about the ploughman? Would you have him homeward plodding his weary way still, or would you allow him his motor-bike?'

'I'd admit that he's a special case. But think of the farmers. A lot of them live in dressy villas in the suburbs of country towns, and drive to work like stockbrokers. What could be more squalid than that?'

'I expect they live that way because urged by their wives. But it's true that, as soon as you get away from picnic routes, the countryside has a more and more unfrequented air. Look at the solitude round us now. And the next building we come to is more likely to be a roofless cottage than not. A foreigner might suppose England to be in a terrible state of depopulation. And this abandoned canal adds to the effect powerfully enough.'

'At least it's peaceful. So I suppose we oughtn't to complain.'

Appleby shook his head.

'Peaceful? I'm not sure it isn't faintly sinister. Do you remember Dr Watson saying something about the country being peaceful and secure, and Sherlock Holmes coming back at him with talk of the horrors that the privacy of the rural life can conceal? I expect there's something in it. I've never found that a policeman's lot in London is a particularly happy one. But it's probably worse in Little Puddleton. Hullo, here's a lock.'

Although with every appearance of neglect and decay, the lock performed its essential function still. Its dark rectangle of water, filmed with green, was several feet higher than the level of the canal on the down-falling side.

'They built these things pretty well for eternity,' Appleby said. 'Look at those dressed stone sides. And what a tremendous invention a lock is! One of those utterly simple things it really takes a great brain to get round to. I expect they first thought of it in China.'

'I think I've read that Leonardo da Vinci was a dab at the things. But perhaps he only cribbed them.' Judith began to walk along one of the gates as she spoke. 'It doesn't just invite one to a dip.'

'Then be careful, for pity's sake. That wood's slimy and treacherous.'

'Nonsense!' Judith said. She increased the boldness of her advance.

'Very well. But if you must fall in, be good enough to do it on the canal side. If you tumble into the lock, it's not very clear to me how I'm to haul you out. And plunging in to the rescue wouldn't help much, either. Two bloated bodies, floating face up, is what the next wayfarer might find to entertain him.'

'Who'd be married to a policeman?' Judith did now make a rather careful retreat. 'Your imagination has been shockingly conditioned by your long frequentation of the morgue. I think I'm rather hungry. Let's push on.'

They went forward as rapidly as the state of the towpath allowed. It was a still day in early summer, and as the little valley drew in around them they seemed to be cut off from the least murmur of sound. Only once or twice there was a *plop!* that sent Judith scanning the surface of the canal for the wake of a water-rat. Scroop House was now well behind them, and Appleby wondered whether his wife might, by good fortune, forget about it. He had some hopes of the tunnel.

And the tunnel – or at least the entrance to it – certainly held a considerable impressiveness. The canal had simply to disappear into a low hill, much as a railway line might do. But the canal had been constructed in the eighteenth century, before such operations took on a merely functional air. The mouth of the tunnel, therefore, was an orifice handsomely framed in a wall of heavily rusticated stone, and even more handsomely embellished with caryatids, herms, cornucopias and a balustrade, while the classical expertness of those responsible for its construction was further attested by a Latin inscription of considerable length and fortunate illegibility.

'It's much more ornate than Scroop House,' Judith said.

'Much.' Appleby was disappointed by this train of thought.

'I expect the owner will tell us about it all.'

'The owner? Tell us about it?'

'The man living at Scroop House will tell us about the canal.'

'He probably knows nothing about it – or about any other local thing. He'll be a City gent, swathed in Old School ties and bogus rurality. And if you insist on making his acquaintance, he'll turn up on you inopportunely in London and ruin one of your gayest and cleverest artistic parties.'

Luckily, perhaps, Judith hadn't listened to this thrust. She was scrambling nearer to the mouth of the tunnel.

'But it hasn't got a towpath!' she cried. 'And they didn't have engines, did they? However did they get the barges through?'

'Leggers.'

'Leggers?'

'Just that. Men who lay on their back on the decks and did the job with their feet. A kind of walking motion on the roof of the tunnel. They must have been pretty flat out by the time they'd done three miles. That's why there's a pub at the end of the tunnel. No doubt there's one at the other end too. By the way, I suppose there's *still* a pub? It didn't shut up shop when the last leggers departed? The idea doesn't bear thinking of. I need lager badly.'

But Judith wasn't alarmed by the possibility of drought. She was now peering into the darkness of the tunnel.

'I wonder if one can go through?' she said. 'You see, they haven't fenced it off in any way. That means it must be safe, don't you think?'

Privately, Appleby thought that it meant just that. But he wasn't sure that he ought to encourage Judith in thoughts of navigation. Not that there wasn't a certain enticingness in the idea, since an adventure of this character would surely sink Scroop House for good.

'I don't see any craft,' he said. 'But perhaps you could wade. I doubt whether you'd be up to your waist in the canal as it is now. Of course, there would be bats.'

'I'm not afraid of bats.'

'Of course not – or not in the open air. But you must remember them as rather uncomfortable companions in a dark room. A three-mile tunnel might be worse. Statistically, I'd say it was almost certain that one of them would get tangled in your hair.'

'Very well.' Judith turned away, admitting defeat. 'I shan't go – ever.'

Appleby laughed as they moved off in search of the pub.

'I'm sure you won't,' he said. 'Nor shall I.'

Chapter Two

Although the last of the leggers must have found rest from his topsyturvy labours many generations ago, the hostelry in which they had recruited themselves was still a going concern. The Applebys established themselves on a bench in the open air and unwrapped their sandwiches. Appleby went inside and returned with beer.

'Did you ask about Scroop House?' Judith said.

'Yes, I did.' Appleby knew very well that, had he failed to do so, he would have been sent back to make good the omission. 'But the chap seems to know nothing about it. New to the place, he said. And he's not the old sort of inn-keeper. R.A.F. type, with a handle-bar moustache specially grown to tell you so. Put in by the brewery company, I suppose, and not very pleased that he hasn't been given a superior little riverside hotel on the lower Thames.'

'I could have told you that without going inside.'

'Could you, indeed?' Appleby thought for a moment and then turned to glance at the door of the pub. There, as the law required, was a legend informing the world that David Channing-Kennedy was licensed to sell spirits, wines and tobacco. 'You're quite right, of course. Truly rural innkeepers don't run to double-barrelled names any more than to that sort of whisker. I always said you ought to be a detective.'

'Elementary, my dear –' Judith broke off and lowered her voice. 'Look,' she said. 'Here's somebody much more hopeful.'

This was certainly true. An old man had emerged from

the door of the public bar, and was looking around him as if in search of a bench on which to sit. In one hand he was carrying something with care. His clothes, which were threadbare but decent, were not particularly rural. Indeed, there was something faintly foreign about them. But it was otherwise with his features. Browned and wizened, these were English and of the folk. But they had a certain fineness, too, and they had not lost sensitiveness in what now appeared to be almost extreme old-age.

'Good morning, sir. Good morning, madam.' The old man had touched a rather battered hat as he spoke. His speech, like his clothes, was distinguishably tinged with strangeness. And now, with his free hand, he made a slight gesture towards a bench a little way from that on which the Applebys sat. He was asking permission to sit down. But this was courtesy and not servility. It gave him, somehow, the air of stepping out of a past age – an age of gentle and simple, master and man.

'Good morning,' Appleby said. 'There's some real warmth in this sun.'

'But you won't have found it too hot for walking. The season's yet a kindly one for that, sir.' The old man sat down, and set his burden carefully beside him. It revealed itself as a beautifully fashioned model of a canal barge – but battered and dusty, as if it had ceased to give anybody pleasure long ago. Judith got up and walked over to it. She had known at once that this was something that would give pleasure now.

'What a lovely thing!' she said. 'A barge seems rather commonplace, when just glanced at. But your model isn't like that. Is it very old?'

'Not older than myself, madam. For it was as a lad that I made it. Not overmuch skill had then come to me. And yet I like it well enough, and thank you for taking notice of it.'

'And you've always had it?' Appleby asked. He had risen and strolled over too.

'Nay – that I haven't. It was for the innkeeper's lass that I fashioned it, and with love-liking enough in the making. But was she Bess or was she Kate? That, now, I disremember – although I well remember the working of the wood. It's the craft that is long in this life, surely, and not how a boy's fancy is moved for a girl.' The old man was now dusting his barge with a clean but frayed and ancient handkerchief. 'But the lass was careless of it, and set it straightway on the chimney-piece in the public bar. So by that I knew she was not for me.'

'But you didn't take back your love-token?' Judith asked. Appleby could see that his wife was much impressed by this Thomas-Hardy-like rural character. 'You let it be?'

'Yes, madam, I let it be. And there it rested, it seems, come many a year, while I myself was wandering. Yet some must have handled it – and let it fall too, which can't, in a public, be thought of as surprising. The rudder is broken, as you can see, and I'd best fashion a new one.'

'Yes, I can see that. But have you the right sort of wood?'

'There's always something in a man's pocket, madam, if his fancy is for work of that kind.' And at once the old man substantiated this claim by producing both a piece of wood and a pocket-knife of the many-bladed variety. 'Cedar, madam, will answer very well. And, by your leave, I'll begin straightway. For there's always hurt in the sight of a broken thing.'

'But you haven't thought of mending it before now?' Appleby asked.

For a moment the old man seemed to hesitate, so that Appleby wondered whether he had been too curious. Then he spoke frankly enough.

'It was but yesterday, sir, that I returned to these parts – my native parts, as you'll have gathered – on account of having a fancy to lay my bones here. Fifteen years I've been from home, working as a carpenter in the city of Spokane –

which one of your knowledge won't fail to know is in the state of Washington, and as far across America as a man may travel.'

'You've certainly come a long way home. And you've always been a carpenter by trade?'

'Never, sir, in a proper manner of speaking, seeing that I was never rightly apprenticed to the trade. Odd lad and handy man I was – that and no more until the sad fancy to emigrate laid hold on me. Yet that there were things above that that I could do is a word to be spoken without overmuch boasting.'

'Would it have been at the big house that you were first employed?' It was with a sudden quickening of interest that Judith asked this.

'Yes, indeed, madam. At Scroop House, and in the old mistress's time.'

'There have been changes since then?'

'Changes more than one, madam – as is but to be expected with time flowing by.' The old man was now busily employed on his piece of cedar-wood, using with a fine dexterity a single slender blade. His employment, Appleby reflected, had the odd effect of rendering entirely agreeable the rather sententious vein of talk he seemed to favour. Conceivably, since he had been away for so long, he was making a conscious effort to recover an almost forgotten manner of speaking. 'Changes there have been, and changes there must be.' It was almost as if the old man were obligingly confirming Appleby in this speculation. 'But those to come will not be of my seeing.' For a moment he put down his knife in order to touch with sensitive fingers the little barge on the bench beside him. 'For as I was saying, sir, it's the craft that's long.'

'We must learn more from him,' Judith said firmly. The Applebys had strolled away again to take another look at the mouth of the tunnel. 'Do you think, if we had another drink ourselves, we might offer him one too?'

'I think we might – and that he would no doubt accept it. His seems to be a case of a rather odd form of nostalgia. He once had something that was known as his place. Now he wants to have it again, just as part of the old days he's come home in search of. If I fetched him out a tankard he'd stand up and ask leave to drink your health in it. And you, of course, would comport yourself in a highly becoming way. Then, quite casually, you would refer to me as "Sir John", fondly supposing that the old chap would become more communicative once he could start saying "my lady" or "your ladyship".'

'Fondly?' Lady Appleby, thus taxed, was entirely unabashed.

'Almost certainly. He's a sensitive old person – a rustic endowed with some undeveloped artistry or the like – and he'll close up at once if he suspects that you're trying to buy something from him for a casual pint, or to come it over him on the strength of being nothing more than London gentry.'

'But he seems quite communicative.'

'My guess is that you deceive yourself, if you think so. As a matter of fact, the venerable old man has something to hide.'

'Something to hide, John? What on earth makes you think that?'

'Thirty years as a policeman. At least he's uncertain about something. And it's not merely that he hasn't yet shaken down into an old environment he's largely forgotten about. There's something more. Perhaps he's even aware that he's been spied on.'

'Spied on? What an outrageous interpretation to put on my quite natural – '

'No, no – I don't mean your mere fishing for information

about your blessed Scroop House. You can go on some way farther there before he closes down – although eventually close down he will. He really *is* being spied on. You see the path we came by, and how it goes on behind that out-building?'

'Yes. It looks like an old stable.'

'Just that. Well, while we were talking, I glimpsed out of the corner of my eye somebody slip rapidly behind it. Whoever it was must then have got inside the stable, because the door facing this way was pushed open just a fraction. The spy was peering out at us.'

'Exactly, John. At *us*.' Judith was laughing. 'We're quite reasonable objects of rural curiosity – probably on the part of a child.'

Appleby shook his head.

'I don't think it was a child – although I couldn't say whether it was man or woman. And I doubt whether a child would spy like that. He would simply stand at a safe distance and openly gape.'

'Well, if it was a grown-up, I rather agree that it would be our old man who was being peered at. This is a pretty quiet part of the world, and any former inhabitant returning from foreign parts is bound to cause quite a stir.'

'That's true enough, and I don't suppose we're in contact with anything sinister. Heaven forbid. I've no taste for a busman's holiday. The thing was oddly furtive, all the same. I think we'll walk round and take a look at that stable.'

This didn't prove difficult. There was an open door at the back. They went in, paused to accustom their eyes to a half-darkness, and then crossed over to another door that Appleby indicated. He gave it a gentle push, so that a tiny crack of light appeared.

'Have a look,' he said.

Judith had a look. And there, sure enough, neatly framed

and in bright sunshine, was the old man, absorbed in his task. It was an entirely peaceful and harmless sight. Yet something about it made her draw back.

'He looks rather helpless,' she said. 'Or unsuspecting. But what could there really be that he ought to be suspicious of? You're making me imagine things. Let's go back and talk to him. And then go back along the canal, cross it at the first lock, and walk up to the big house.'

They returned to the front of the inn. Judith sat down beside the old man, and for some time watched him at work in silence.

'Perhaps,' she said casually, 'you know Colonel Raven of Pryde Park?'

'Yes, madam. He has been a prominent man in these parts these many years. And a famous fisherman.'

'We have walked over from Pryde Park. Colonel Raven is my uncle. I want you to tell me more about Scroop House.'

For a moment the old man ignored this. He had ducked his head in the rural equivalent of a polite bow.

'It wouldn't by any chance,' he said, 'be Miss Judith Raven I'm speaking to – the lady that married the great policeman?'

Judith was startled. When young she had frequently visited her Uncle Julius. But to be enshrined in local memory in a countryside not her own was altogether surprising.

'Yes,' she said. 'My name is Appleby now. And this is my husband, Sir John. But I don't think many people round about here would recall me.'

'Happen not, my lady. But I'm a remembering man. I remember much about Scroop House in the old days, and a little about Pryde Park too. But the Park, asking your pardon, was of little mark compared with the House. Ravens, I know well, have never been common folk, but their

20

uncommonness has been most by way of strangeness, more often than not.'

'Quite true,' Appleby broke in with some emphasis. 'My wife's people are an eccentric crowd. But in rather a distinguished way. Scroop House must have been quite a place in those old days, if it cast the Colonel and his remarkable activities into the shade. What was so striking about it?'

'Mrs Coulson herself, sir.' The old man's voice had turned oddly vibrant, as if years had dropped from him as he spoke. 'There are few fine ladies like her nowadays. And in the big house, my lady, everything from cellar to attic of a fineness that answered to her. And the house-parties, my lady! They were no matter merely of county folk. No – there was far more than mere gentry eager to gather round Mrs Coulson. Great men from Parliament came. And others above them, again. Poets, my lady, and great artists and deep philosophers. They called Mrs Coulson – her friends did – the Grand Collector. And it was a joke that was meant all in an admiring way. For Mrs Coulson had nowise to go out and gather people in. Thronging they came to her, the most brilliant in the land. Beautiful women, my lady, and handsome men – and all in a setting she had made worthy of them. Perhaps there were many other such houses in England then, such as a poor man like myself had no knowledge of. But Scroop House was enough for me, and proud I was to serve it.'

'It does sound very splendid.' Judith spoke gently after a pause. She knew that there must be some exaggeration in the old man's picture, since otherwise she would have heard of these neighbouring glories at some time from her uncle. But of the genuineness of the enthusiasm behind the description there could be no doubt. The finely carved little barge now lay neglected on the bench. The old man was sitting with kindled face and idle hands.

'But at Mrs Coulson's death' – Appleby asked – 'all the glory departed? And you departed too?'

'That is true, sir. Scroop went to a distant cousin of the mistress – a stranger who never so much as came to look at it, but instantly rented it out, all fine as it was, to a mere moneyed man from London, a Mr Binns – to whom William Chambers, my lady, who your ladyship will know built Scroop, meant no more than some common name. I stayed on for a time – no more than an outside man as I was – and then the heartbreak of it was too much for me, and to America, my lady, I departed.'

'But what a shame!'

Judith Appleby expressed this sentiment with great conviction. Her husband said nothing. Ever so slightly, this old person puzzled him. Judith, clearly, was accepting him as a mute, inglorious Milton – an artist *manqué*. And Appleby told himself that it was only his own long career as an inglorious Sherlock Holmes, a professional sifter of every sort of knavery, that disposed him to the feeling that the old man was playing some sort of part. Either he was doing that – Appleby said to himself – or he was perhaps covering up something that had recently disconcerted him. There was, indeed, almost nothing in what the old man had said, that could be adduced in support of either of these suppositions. It was simply – as again Appleby told himself – that a lifetime of criminal investigation, even when blunted by a few years of mere high-level police administration, left one at the mercy of hunches, of obscure intimations that here was a little more than met the eye or ear.

'But perhaps' – he said – 'there has now been another change at Scroop House? And that is why you have returned here?'

There was a moment's silence. Then the old man again picked up the little barge, studied it, put it down, and

22

returned to delicately carving the new rudder. When he spoke, it was cautiously and with obvious reserve.

'Well, sir, I wouldn't say it's not so. For there is a Coulson back at Scroop. He is the same gentleman, mark you, that once let the place – lock, stock and barrel – to the Mr Binns that I was telling you of. Mr Bertram Coulson, his name is. And when I heard sir, that he had returned to the old house, just as Mrs Coulson left it, it seemed to me that a change of heart might have come upon him, and that his thought might be to cherish his inheritance, and that I should come home and see for myself.'

'You thought, perhaps, that you might even find employment again under the new owner?'

'Well, sir, I am too old for such to be other than a bold thought in me. But I won't say that it has been altogether absent from my mind.' The old man paused. 'I'd dearly like to settle back here for the short remainder of my days, turning my hand to what I can. For there have been Crabtrees hereabouts for a power of years.'

'You are Mr Crabtree?' Judith asked.

'Yes, my lady. Seth Crabtree.'

'And how is it going?' Judith was delighted that the old man should have a name so appropriate to his rustic character. 'Have you been back to the big house yet?'

'Yes, my lady. It was only this morning that I ventured there.'

'Did you find it much changed?'

Seth Crabtree took time to consider this, and a shadow as of perplexity or caution came over his face as he did so.

'Well, as to the house, my lady, I had but a glimpse of it. I went to the front door, which was perhaps no proper thing for one in my place. But there are small matters that one forgets after long living among other customs in other countries.' Seth Crabtree paused again on this, which represented perhaps the first shade of irony to have entered his studiously respectful speech. And the effect was to suggest some entirely hidden dimension in the man. 'So it came about,' he went on, 'that the door was opened to me by Mr Hollywood himself.'

'Mr Hollywood?' Judith, for some reason, found this name rather odd. 'The owner is called – ?'

'No, indeed. It's a Mr Bertram Coulson, who has always been the owner, who is in residence now.'

'But of course. You explained that to us. And Mr Hollywood is – ?'

'The butler, my lady – although it was early in the day for the butler himself to be performing that duty. It makes me think that perhaps the big house is not staffed as it ought to be.'

'I see.' Judith was properly impressed. 'And you recognized this Mr Hollywood? He is the same butler as in the old days?'

'He is, my lady. And I am told that he is the only man or women – manservant or maidservant, I should say – who has never left the place.'

'And he, on his part, recognized you?'

Again Seth Crabtree showed a shade of perplexity – and perhaps of some less identifiable emotion as well.

'As to that, it would be hard to say. Mr Hollywood gave no sign.'

'But when you told him your name?'

'He was unresponsive, my lady. Perhaps it was natural and to be expected. I was never, remember, more than an outdoor servant about Scroop House. Or but that, at least, in name.' Crabtree fell abruptly silent, as if something had slipped from him without his intending it. At the same time he sheathed his knife and showed some disposition to take his leave.

24

Judith nipped this intention in the bud.

'But Mr Coulson?' she said. 'You asked for him?'

'He was not at home, my lady, but out and about on the business of the estate – a proper thing, that I was glad to hear of. So there I was, with but a glimpse of the hall and its grand staircase, noble places, the same as I remembered them. And yet there was a strangeness that must have come of all those absent years.' Crabtree shook his head broodingly – a perplexed rural philosopher. '*Tempus fugit*, my lady.'

'I expect everything would have rather a strange look for a while. And in fact you have never met the present Mr Coulson?'

'Never, my lady – since I left the big house, as I explained to you, in Mr Binns's time. Or never until today. For I did, after all, meet Mr Coulson – less than a couple of hours ago, and as I was walking across the park, thinking to cross the canal and come to this inn. There the gentleman was, my lady, and he stopped me and spoke to me.'

'And what did you think of him, Mr Crabtree?'

Seth Crabtree now had a more notable hesitation. Perhaps he was only registering a feeling that this was not a wholly proper question to address to one of humble station. Perhaps – on the other hand – he was really in doubt as to how to answer.

'Affable, my lady,' he presently said. 'An affable gentleman. Open and conversable. But not, my lady, what you might call a gentleman after the old style, if you follow me.'

Judith did follow. Seth Crabtree had, in fact, pronounced against the present owner of Scroop House the very terrible verdict that he was not quite as other gentry are. And this was puzzling.

'But surely, Mr Crabtree, even a cousin of old Mrs Coulson's – '

'A distant cousin, my lady, as I remarked. And I believe

he has lived much in foreign parts. And I would guess – if the liberty may be taken – not in the best society. He would scarcely have fitted into one of the mistress's house-parties in times gone by. Not that Scroop House was not open to talent. Very much so, it was. Actresses would come, my lady, and Parliament people from the Labour Party. Yes, indeed. But there would always be about them – ' Seth Crabtree had one of his sudden silences. And this time he got to his feet. 'But Mr Coulson was very kind,' he said. 'He had no occasion to take notice of me. But when I told him how I'd been about the place long ago, he said I was to come and see him at the big house tomorrow, and that he was doing great things around the estate, and that he would see whether there might be work for me.'

'But that's splendid,' Judith said.

'Yes, my lady – even if the work is not Mrs Coulson's work.' Seth Crabtree had been looking critically at his half carved rudder. Now he slipped it into a pocket and put the model barge under his arm. 'There's nobody will mind my borrowing this,' he said. 'And, when the repair's made, it may as well go back to the chimney-piece where it's stood for so long. And now, sir and my lady, I'll take my leave, after having been burdening you overlong with my story. But your interest was kindly, and has been kindly taken.'

'Perhaps we'll see you again soon,' Judith said. 'I hope we do.'

'Thank you kindly again, my lady. And it may be so, for life has many chances.'

And at this, Seth Crabtree gave his bob of a bow and walked away. He had concluded the meeting, Appleby reflected, very deliberately on the note of the rural sage.

Chapter Three

'We shan't, in fact, see him again,' Appleby said. 'So we'll never quite know about him.'

'Or why he was being spied on. But we shall meet Mr Bertram Coulson. An affable gentleman, even if not quite in the old style. Open and conversable. Mark that, John. We only have to go up to Scroop House, announce that the work of William Chambers fascinates us, and sit down in the middle of it. Hollywood will then be summoned, and the cake and Madeira will appear. We'll go now.'

It hadn't occurred to Appleby that Judith would thus see as a green light Seth Crabtree's description of the owner of the big house. But now, to his satisfaction, what was at least a momentary distraction turned up. It took the form of the appearance from the inn of that Mr David Channing-Kennedy who advertised himself as licensed to sell spirits, wines, beers and tobacco in its interior. He was of a muscular frame beginning to run to flesh; his complexion was florid; his huge handle-bar moustache, presumably the cherished symbol of a martial past, was of a bright ginger hue. His clothes would have been best described as sporty, their elements being so mingled that their owner might with equal propriety have been about to jump on a horse, lurk behind a butt, pant after a pack of beagles, or wade in quest of trout or salmon deep into the flood.

'Good afternoon.' Mr Channing-Kennedy addressed Judith with the confidence proper in an equal, and the cordiality – at once measured and easy – of a hotelier skilled in the higher reaches of his trade. At the same time he gave

Appleby, rather oddly, a glance a good deal sharper than he had favoured him with on their earlier encounter in the inn. 'A splendid day for walking, is it not? Can I get you anything more? Coffee, perhaps? We do manage rather tolerable coffee, although it seems not much in demand in these parts.'

'No, thank you,' Judith said. And she added: 'You haven't been here long?'

'No, no – not for long. Terrible blighters, you know, the chaps who run chains of pubs like this. But even they wouldn't keep me on a permanent assignment down here. The idea is that the place should be pulled together. That it should be worked up, you know, in the direction of a better class of trade. There's accommodation for the night, of course, although only in a small way. I'm working that up too. We rather hope for tourists in the season. The Company is putting out publicity about the Canal and the tunnel. The tunnel's rather unique in its way. Constructed in the medieval period or thereabouts' – and Mr Channing-Kennedy waved a hand as if to excuse himself from the pursuit of any pedantic chronological nicety – 'and over three miles long. Wonderful what those old chaps could do. Cathedrals, and so forth. All by hand. Flint arrows and stone axes, now. Remarkable things, eh? Small brains, and all that, as the pundits can tell by the shape of the skulls. Puny too, in a way. Look at the suits of armour in the museums. The outfits of famous knights, eh? And yet you could hardly get an undersized Pay Corps boy into one of them today. All because we're tolerably well provided at the trough nowadays. Even the plebs – eh? Live like lords. Live a damned sight too high, if you ask me. And not even content with it. Reds at heart, the whole lot of them. Need discipline. And another big show would bring that fast enough, whatever else it brought. What they call a balance of advantages. A loud bang or two, but the whole unruly crowd put on parade.'

Mr. Channing-Kennedy, as he talked this disagreeable nonsense, was still favouring Appleby from time to time with an appraising glance. And the appraisal struck Appleby as of an order cooler and more collected than was altogether congruous with Mr Channing-Kennedy's woolly talk. In part, moreover, it was a kind of glance with which Appleby, like other men of a mild celebrity, was familiar: the kind of glance that is comparing a living and present image with a recollected photograph. Since serving Appleby with beer it had occurred to Mr Channing-Kennedy that here was a face somehow familiar to him. He had even perhaps identified it. But this scarcely seemed to justify something wary in his rather covert scrutiny. Perhaps Mr Channing-Kennedy did not possess the comfort of an entirely clear conscience in minor matters of the law. But – although he scarcely seemed a very intelligent man – he could hardly suppose that he was being run to earth by London's Commissioner of Metropolitan Police in person.

Talk now seemed likely to languish, since Appleby was not one largely given to casual conversation and Judith was distinctly unsympathetic to the philosophical propositions to which this dubiously *déclassé* publican adhered. But for a further minute or two Mr Channing-Kennedy talked on – although with so little encouragement that Appleby found himself wondering whether the fellow had some motive for detaining them. Was he proposing to fish for information? Was he – conceivably – anxious that Seth Crabtree should be well out of the way before his late interlocutors should be free to trail him? These were fantastic conjectures. They were a throwback – Appleby found himself reflecting – to his old C.I.D. days, when a large part of his waking life had been dominated by the supposition that there was a crook in every second citizen he encountered. This Channing-Kennedy was a vulgar and rather offensive fellow, but there was not the slightest real reason to believe that he was in any such category – any more than there had been any real reason to believe that there was more in Seth Crabtree than Judith had been disposed to remark in him.

And yet there was another queer thing about the unengaging Channing-Kennedy. Half his mind was on what might be called his lines of communication. The canal was no longer a real artery; nothing arrived at or departed from the inn by this route any more. Wayfarers, indeed, might come along the towpath, as Appleby himself and Judith had done. But this would be at the cost of laddered stockings and muddy trousers. As Appleby had remarked, in a motorized age people were no longer disposed to potter along the bank of a canal. The normal approach to the inn was now by a lane at the back: a narrow and winding affair, barely adequate for vehicular traffic, which presumably led to some more commodious highway along which Channing-Kennedy's anticipated cohorts of tourists would advance. Conceivably his uneasily divided attention at this moment was to be attributed to the expectation that the great moment had come. Alternatively, he might simply be afraid that something awkward was due to turn up. Perhaps he ran a side-line, unknown to the respectable firm of brewers that employed him, in the purveying of illicit liquors. This retired spot was at some remove from the sea – although the canal had, indeed, once led to it directly. But perhaps it was known to Channing-Kennedy that a band of confederate smugglers was even now approaching, roaring profane and bawdy songs as they convoyed to the inn whole hogsheads of rum.

Involved in this fantasy, Appleby was by a few seconds tardy in realizing that a vehicle was now approaching the inn in sober fact. There was indeed a rumble, a screech of brakes, and the shutting off of a rather noisy engine before he turned and saw what had arrived. It was less a large van than a young pantechnicon, and it could certainly be carrying enough rum to inebriate the whole county. And the driver, as he climbed from the cab and came forward, did reveal himself as one who would have made a highly convincing smuggler in some melodrama or *opera bouffe* of the seaboard. He was hairy and ill-favoured, and he wore a scowl which darkened to deep suspicion as he stared at Appleby. Then he turned to Channing-Kennedy and stared at him too. Channing-Kennedy stared back at him. Appleby had an impression that for a second both men were at a loss.

'I've brought yer pianer,' the sullen man said ferociously. He jerked a thumb at his van. 'Crated, it is. Got a couple of men to give a hand with a bleeding crated pianer? Weighs a bleeding ton. Sending out a man single-handed with a bleeding pianer! I asks yer.'

'A piano, you great fool?' Channing-Kennedy appeared to be highly indignant. His complexion, growing even more florid, glowed like a bonfire behind the enormous ginger moustache. And Appleby glanced at him curiously. His uncompromising disapproval of the plebs had, of course, already declared itself. But it seemed odd that he should venture to address a particularly hulking stranger from among them in so brutally opprobrious a way.

'A piano, you idiot?' Channing-Kennedy seemed to throw this in for good measure. 'I'm not expecting a piano. What should I want a piano for? To play myself to sleep with Mozart and that crowd?' Channing-Kennedy gave a short, sharp bellow of laughter on this, so that one had to suppose he considered it a considerable witticism. 'What place do you take this for, anyway? The Royal Albert Hall?' Channing-Kennedy gave another bellow of laughter. But his glance, Appleby thought, was curiously hard.

The smuggler had produced a grubby sheet of paper which was presumably a way-bill. He studied it. He was breathing hard – perhaps out of justified indignation, perhaps merely as a consequence of having to bring an uncertain degree of literacy to bear on the document. He mumbled something in which the word 'House' could just be distinguished.

'Nonsense!' Channing-Kennedy said. 'Can't you see that this is an inn? Don't they give you a map? You're miles out of your way. Go back to the village and ask the old woman in the post-office. She's as deaf as a post.' Once more, Channing-Kennedy bellowed with laughter. 'You can play her a sonata by one of those rotten old Krauts. Beethoven, eh? Now, be off with you. And see you do no damage when you turn in my yard.'

The smuggler said nothing more. He was still breathing stertorously. He just gave Channing-Kennedy a long look – and received a long look in return. He lumbered over to his van, climbed in, and manoeuvred it, to the accompaniment of much clashing of gears, in the confined space before the inn. Then he departed as he had come. The lane was narrow and its surface deplorable. The piano must have been suffering badly.

Appleby had picked up his rucksack. Mr Channing-Kennedy, he felt, was a person to whom it would be rather nice to say good-bye. But the sight of the van making its way with difficulty up the narrow lane prompted Judith to a question.

'I suppose,' she asked, 'it was the canal that was the chief approach to your inn at one time?'

'That was the jolly old idea, of course.' And Channing-Kennedy nodded in rather a distracted manner. 'There were coaching inns, you know, and there were canal inns as well. The coaching inns got a second innings' – and Channing-

Kennedy bellowed in tribute to this striking pun – 'when the motor-car came along. But most of the canal inns were knocked out by the railways. A few just kept going, and this is one of them. Not that this one wasn't shut down for a good many years. Something bogus about it, if you ask me.' Channing-Kennedy said this with the large severity of one to whom the spurious is abhorrent in every way. 'It's name, for instance. Invented by my damned brewery company no time ago at all. The sign's away being painted' – he had followed Judith's glance – 'so you wouldn't know. But it's called the Jolly Leggers. Silly, eh? Precious little they had to be jolly about – lying on their backs on the bally barges and doing their treadmill turn on the roof of the tunnel. Not that they'd be other than a sort of scum fit for nothing else. Plenty of that sort nowadays, too – eh?'

Judith ignored this appeal, but still sought information.

'Does anybody use parts of the canal any longer? There seems to be a certain amount of water in this section still. And the last lock we passed seemed almost in working order.'

'Anybody use it? Good Lord, no! You could get a punt or dinghy along stretches of it, I suppose. But who'd want to do that? Dreary thing a canal, I'd say. Of course the tunnel is different.' Channing-Kennedy appeared to recollect this suddenly. 'Historical interest, and all that – as I was saying. Tourists sure to come along when the publicity boys do their stuff.'

'Are you going to take them for trips in the tunnel? Can one go through?'

'*Through* the tunnel?' The landlord of the Jolly Leggers was horrified. 'Lord, no! Damned dangerous place. Falling masonry. Foul air. Death trap, absolutely.'

'But I see it's not shut off in any way. Are the local children never tempted to explore it?'

Channing-Kennedy chuckled unpleasantly.

T – A.C.C. – B

'I'd take the hide off their bottoms if they tried. The place is my Company's property now, you see. But, in fact, the brats don't go near it. Got a bad name. Haunted, the locals think. Some legend or old wives' tale about it, I believe. Ignorant crowd, the yokels round about here. But uppish, too. Think they know a thing or two about beer.'

'And do they?' Appleby asked.

'As a matter of fact, old boy, I'd rather suppose they do.' Channing-Kennedy, as he used this abominable form of address, seemed to have a moment of simple candour. 'And I know damn-all about it myself. Scotch and gin see me through the day – with a drop of brandy at shut-eye, when this hole looks like getting me down. The Channing-Kennedys have been short drinkers for a good many generations, I'd say.' Mr David Channing-Kennedy advanced this proud claim with all the casual seriousness of a man intimating a long family connexion with the Quorn or the Brigade of Guards. 'Going on your way, are you? Well, chin-chin!'

'What a dreadful man,' Judith said as they walked off. 'And I suppose his kind are pushing out the decent old pub-keepers all over the place.'

'I rather doubt that. I don't suppose there are all that number of Channing-Kennedys around. Or, on the other hand, all that number of Seth Crabtrees. All in all, this seems to me to be rather an odd part of the world.'

Judith laughed.

'You get ideas in your head, John. It's a trick of the old sage. You'd like to stumble on a mystery, busman's holiday or no busman's holiday. I suppose that the van driver was odd too?'

'Oh, most decidedly.' They were now back on the towpath, and Appleby set off along it without hesitation. 'I think this will be our shortest way.'

'Our shortest way?' Judith was puzzled. 'Back to Pryde Park?'

'Certainly not. On to Scroop House.'

'Scroop House!' Judith was so astonished that she stopped in her tracks.

'Isn't that where you want to go? Have you forgotten your glass of Madeira with Mr Bertram Coulson? Open and affable, he will see at a glance that the Ravens have been short drinkers even longer than the Channing-Kennedys. So there you'll be, my lady. And I shall be accommodated with a mug of ale in the butler's pantry by Mr Hollywood.'

Judith found it unnecessary to respond to this pleasantry. For some minutes she walked on in silence. John, she told herself, being aware that she was determined to take him to Scroop House, was rather childishly proposing to take the wind out of her sails by asserting that *he* was determined to take *her*. But, no – she knew quite well that this wasn't it. John's curiosity about places and people was quite different from hers. And something had brought it into play. On a country walk, for instance, he would stride beside her for most of the time in an abstraction. Perhaps he was brooding on London's traffic problems or on the latest statistics of juvenile crime. She wouldn't know. And then from time to time he would emerge and talk about anything that came into his head. But it was she who noticed the lie of the land and read the map. That was how it commonly was. But at this moment, she saw, John was very aware of his surroundings. He had now stopped to take a better look at them. Something had put it into his head to get hold of what he would have called the terrain.

The towpath – as they had discovered on their outward walk – was muddy, crumbling and overgrown. But Judith found a log, sat on it, and watched John fish out the map. She herself got out a cigarette. She had hardly lit it before John

35

had put on a turn with his watch and the sun, oriented the map by means of some Boy Scout's ensuing calculation, and was holding forth (she thought with ironic affection) like a brigadier impressing his staff on manoeuvres.

'The village near the inn' – Appleby said – 'is no more than a hamlet. It's called Nether Scroop. But a secondary motor-road goes through it, sweeps towards the canal on a gentle curve, comes nearest to it when level with the lock you did that foolish little walk on, and then sweeps away to the south again. Eventually it becomes our own familiar road past Pryde Park.'

'Yes, John,' Judith said.

'As soon as we get to the lock, we have the park of Scroop House on our left, across the canal. The house itself stands a quarter of a mile back from the canal, and is on the eastern fringe of the park proper. On the east, that is to say, one quickly comes to solid beech woods, which run from the canal to the high road north of the house.'

'Yes, John. As a matter of fact, I can see them from here.'

'From the house to the canal there's some sort of track indicated on the map. It ends at what may be an old wharf. That's interesting. If you ask me, canal and house came into being more or less together – and the canal was the real artery to the grand house, just as much as to the humble inn farther west. It wasn't an uncommon set-up. The gentry – Ravens and the like – drove up by road in post-chaises and barouches and what-have-you. But the coal and the provender – to say nothing of the building materials in the first place – arrived by the wonderful new canal. It's true that the house now looks as if it had been built rather close to a whacking great high road. But, in fact, there can have been little more than a lane. The big road to the north of the house, that's to say, which runs roughly parallel to the canal, belongs to an altogether later age. And it's had the effect of squashing the village of Upper Scroop between itself and Scroop House. To the north, the house almost turns into village. No doubt the village nestles in an appropriately humble and protected and over-lorded way beneath the house. But the effect of spaciousness and privacy is all on the side of the park – here, that's to say, to the south.'

'It's private enough. As we were saying, this countryside seems absolutely deserted. Not a sign of habitation, population, a trace of the modern world.'

'You're wrong there, Judith. Look South.'

Judith looked south – which was towards what Appleby had called the secondary motor-road. All she saw was a momentary glint of light.

'I think,' she said, 'that I saw the sun reflected from the windscreen of a passing car. Right?'

'Right as far as you go. What you saw was a silver-grey Rolls-Royce Phantom V.'

'My dear John, it's terribly vulgar to *name* cars – particularly astoundingly expensive ones. It's only done by cheap novelists. You must say: "a very large car".'

Appleby received this with hilarity.

'It isn't' – he said – 'for that matter so *very* large. There are American cars you could pretty well tuck it into the boot or trunk of. But I agree that it's in the upper income bracket. Somebody rather comfortably off is frequenting these rural near-solitudes.'

'Perhaps it's Mr Bertram Coulson. Perhaps he's put into a really terrific car the money that should be hiring phalanxes of footmen to relieve Hollywood of the invidious task of answering the front-door bell at improper hours. But what's the point of getting interested in a passing car, anyway?'

Appleby shook his head.

'I don't know,' he said. 'I just don't know, at all. Let's

walk on.' He glanced again at the map. 'We'll cross the canal by the lock. That's not very far from what I said might be a wharf on the Scroop House side. There's probably a track to it along the canal. And then we can take the old road up through the park to the house.'

'Again we're not in utter solitude, after all,' Judith said. 'But this time it's not a Rolls. It's a wayfarer. And actually coming towards us, along the towpath.'

'Somebody for you to pass the time of day with. Perhaps he can tell us –' Appleby broke off. 'Well, I'm blessed!'

'Whatever is it now?'

'Didn't you see the fellow stop?'

'Of course I saw him stop. What of it? Whoever he is, he's coming on again now.'

'Only because he realizes that we've seen him. *He* saw *us* – and came to a momentary dead halt. Isn't that odd?'

'Not in the least.' Judith said this not wholly confidently. 'He's one of those pathologically shy people who would walk round the block rather than encounter their oldest friend. They often take to rambling and bird-watching and so forth. It seems to me, incidentally, that you're going a shade pathological yourself. Paranoia. Suspecting things.'

Appleby ignored this.

'He doesn't look like a bird-watcher,' he said. 'I'd guess that he was the local doctor.'

'Very well. He's the local doctor, going his rounds.'

'But he hasn't got one of those little bags. And where are the patients? Nothing but cows round about here.'

'Then perhaps he's the local vet. Let's ask him.'

'I wouldn't put it beyond you. But I don't think he's going to give us much opportunity for chat. Just a civil but unpausing good day.'

This forecast proved to be correct. The stranger – who, although in country tweeds, did give the impression of being a professional man not far from his job – brushed past the Applebys on the narrow path with only a curt greeting.

'There you are,' Appleby said, when they were out of hearing. 'He wouldn't – would he? – recognize us again if he saw us. The look he gave us was just that sort of look. Projecting upon *us*, you know, what he'd like to think held of himself. A simple and very common psychological mechanism.'

'John, for pity's sake! Don't be such a *bore*.' Judith didn't, in fact, look at all bored. She was amused. 'You mean he'd like to think we might see him again tomorrow and not know him from Adam?'

'Just that.'

'This mystery-mongering is beyond me. Thank heavens it comes on you only in spasms.'

'Very well. And now for Mr and Mrs Bertram Coulson.'

'Seth Crabtree didn't mention Bertram Coulson's having a wife.'

'No – but then, for Seth Crabtree, there has been only one woman in the world. Barring, that is, the girl who wasn't interested in the barge he carved for her. Only *the* Mrs Coulson, the Grand Collector, counts with him. Incidentally, we didn't gather if *she* had a husband in Seth's time. But, as I say, now for Mr and Mrs Bertram Coulson and the children.'

'Children?'

'I see no reason why Scroop House shouldn't be normally accommodated in that way. Instead of seed-cake and Madeira, a jolly family tea. And here's the lock. Just be careful getting across the gate. It's slippery. And, as I said before, if you go in, it won't be easy to get you out. Or to get help, for that matter. It's an uncommonly lonely spot.'

'Why are men so fond of telling women to be careful?' As she spoke, Judith was examining the lock gates. 'You know, they haven't the look of being kept in any sort of repair. And yet I think they could be made to open. And the ones at the other end, too.'

'That's so.' Putting a hand lightly on an insecure and rotting breast-rail, Appleby peered down into the lock, as he had done on their outward walk. 'Hullo! Something seems to have come to the surface.' He stiffened. 'Judith – are you across?'

Judith laughed. 'Yes, John. Safe on the bank, thank you.'

'Then I can tell you something rather shocking. I'm afraid it's a body.' He paused. 'It's Seth Crabtree,' he said quietly.

Chapter Four

Judith came back at once and stood beside Appleby on the gate. She was pale, but she looked down steadily at the inert form in the lock. It lay prone, so that the face was invisible. But the clothes were certainly Crabtree's. And Crabtree's battered old hat floated nearby.

'John – do you think he's dead?'

'It looks like that, I'm afraid. But I must get down and see. Perhaps we can revive him.'

As he spoke, Appleby got to his knees on the gate, lowered himself over its edge, dropped to the full stretch of his arms, and then let himself fall. It wasn't a particularly hazardous operation, but it was a messy one. He expected a good deal of mud beneath the few feet of water, and there was in fact enough of it to suck in an ugly way at his legs as he strove to retain his balance after the drop. Laboriously, he waded the few feet that separated him from the body.

'Face submerged,' he called up to Judith. 'He's suspended somehow – or sprawled on a snag of some sort. No – it's his coat that has caught on the hinge of the gate. That's prevented him from going right under. There may be some hope. I think I can turn him over.' He bent over the body, and Judith heard a stifled exclamation.

'What is it, John?'

'He's caught himself a very queer crack. I don't like it. And I can't do much down here. So we're faced with what we were talking about: the problem of getting out. Go to the other gate – will you? – and see if, by any chance, the sluice or valve or whatever it's called is working. If we can get the level down and the gates open, then I can lug him into the canal at that end, and we can manage some sort of scramble up the bank.'

Judith did as she was told.

'No go,' she called, almost at once. 'There isn't a handle to crank the thing with.'

'Just cast around. It may have been chucked aside and be covered with grass or something.'

'You're right.' Judith spoke again almost at once. 'I've found it. And it fits. And it's working.' She paused, and Appleby could hear her winding vigorously. 'The water's going out, all right. But there may be too much mud on the bottom for me to budge the gate. Can you come and tug at it while I shove.'

'Yes – but I'll have to bring Crabtree with me. And rust may beat us, as well as mud. If the hinges are stuck fast, then you'll just have to go for help. Delay won't harm me. But it will spoil any slim chance this poor devil may have.'

Judith felt that John's tone conveyed a fuller knowledge about Seth Crabtree than his words did. And the grim task of extrication went on. The gates did move – surprisingly easily. And the inert body was eventually got up on the bank. It oughtn't, they knew, to have been manhandled at all before medical aid was summoned. But in the circumstances there seemed no help for it.

'If the man who passed us on the towpath was really the local doctor,' Judith said, 'perhaps one of us ought to go after him.'

'And perhaps it ought to be me.' Appleby was kneeling beside Crabtree as he spoke. 'At the moment I represent the law, after all.'

Judith glanced swiftly at her husband.

'John! You don't mean – ?'

'I mean that the fellow was coming straight from this spot.

42

He may have been the last person to see Crabtree alive. And that's to put it – well, cautiously.'

For a moment Judith didn't take this in.

'Oughtn't we to get the water out of his lungs, and try artificial respiration? I can do the breath technique.'

Appleby shook his head gently. Then, equally gently, he turned Crabtree's head as it lay on the ground. And Judith momentarily recoiled.

'Could it have happened' – she asked in a controlled voice – 'by his striking against something as he fell? I mean, it could be an accident, surely?'

'Yes – upon one condition.' Expertly, Appleby had been feeling for pulse and heart. 'Some pathological fragility of the skull. But it's only a remote possibility. The police surgeon will be able, I imagine, to tell at once. But I can't see *that*' – and Appleby brought out a handkerchief and laid it over the dead man's head – 'as anything other than a deliberate and crushing blow.'

Appleby stood up. He looked at the body. He looked at the open lock gates and frowned. He looked at the line of the disused canal, with its foot or two of water scummed with green. He crossed it again by the still closed gates at the east end, and stepped delicately up and down the towpath, scanning the ground. He returned and did the same on the other bank.

'As I thought,' he said, 'there's a track in the direction of the wharf or shed or whatever it is, farther along.'

Judith didn't seem to hear.

'That we should have stumbled on this,' she said. 'That *you* should.'

'Yes – that *I* should.' And Appleby smiled grimly. 'The local people may feel it to be distinctly off my beat. A kind of gate-crashing – like our proposed pleasant tea with the

43

Bertram Coulsons. That's off, I'm afraid.' Again he looked down at the body. 'The little barge, Judith. It's vanished.'

'Probably it's at the bottom of the lock.'

'It can scarcely be. It would float.'

'Crabtree threw it away. He remembered the girl again with some sudden pain or vividness. And, in a revulsion, he threw away the old love-token.'

'It's a romantic thought. But I think it more probable that somebody has made off with it.'

'Why should anybody do that? Isn't it more mystery-mongering?'

Appleby shook his head.

'My dear – let's face it. This old man, whom we were talking to an hour ago, has been murdered – and by an unknown hand. Would you mind waiting here beside the body?'

'Of course not.'

'Then I'll go back to the inn, and telephone the police.' Appleby picked up his rucksack and produced what seemed to be a second sandwich tin. He opened it and handed a small automatic pistol to his wife. 'A touch of melodrama,' he said. 'But you never know. What the neswpapers call a homicidal maniac may be concerned. And may turn up again.'

Judith took the weapon without comment. She had seen such things before.

Aeroplanes – Appleby said to himself as he walked rapidly back to the Jolly Leggers. Aeroplanes are nowadays extremely elaborate affairs, made up of a great many bits and pieces. Conceivably they shed chunks of metal from time to time, without anybody much noticing. Or again, there are still some quite small aeroplanes, the occupants of which are not hermetically encapsulated, and out of one of these some careless person might simply drop something. So the mud at the bottom of the lock must be searched for anything of the sort. Not that he himself proposed to venture any advice in the matter. The Crabtree affair was very much something he proposed to keep out of. For one thing, he was on holiday. And, for another thing, it would look just too silly in the newspapers. Commissioners of Police simply do not come upon corpses during rural walks. It was another of the things that just aren't done.

Then there was Aeschylus – Appleby continued to reflect. When the eminent dramatist was at an even more advanced age than Seth Crabtree, an eagle dropped a tortoise on his cranium, with fatal results. But although tortoises were no doubt to be found here and there as pets among the children of the peasantry, the concurrent presence of an eagle in the neighbourhood was in the highest degree unlikely. Could there be any other accidental cause of Crabtree's death?

It was not remotely possible that the discharge of a shotgun could produce such a wound as the dead man's head had suffered. Such a weapon can, indeed, do something very nasty to a skull – but it has to be deliberately applied thereto for the purpose. A rifle bullet was a more conceivable agent – but rifles are seldom so employed as to produce accidental slaughter. A strong boy playing with a powerful catapult was a hypothesis not to be neglected. Such a boy could hardly be unaware of what he had achieved. But he might, of course, have fled in panic.

I am going to have nothing to do with this – Appleby repeated to himself, as the inn came in sight and he increased his pace. Nothing at all.

But now suppose – his mind ran on – that Crabtree, despite his years, had for some reason been running at breakneck speed. Had he then stumbled on the lock gate, with

45

the consequence of some impact to the force of which that breakneck speed contributed its additional impetus? Would any very special fragility of bone be needed to account for the damage sustained? I think it still would, he answered himself. And he stode into the inn and demanded the telephone.

And the following two hours found Appleby realizing that, after all, old habit was too strong for him. If only in the quietest way, he was going to be in on the Crabtree mystery. A certain Inspector Hilliard, a taciturn and clearly capable officer who had appeared with commendable promptitude from police headquarters in the county town, was indisposed to regard as other than a satisfactory circumstance that it happened to be Sir John Appleby who had come upon the body. What little he said implied that he would be grateful for any assistance he received. This being so, Appleby couldn't very well withdraw in haste as soon as he had offered what might be called a lay statement of his own knowledge of the affair. He was constrained – as he later put it to Judith – to do a little pottering around in a professional manner. And, as a consequence of this, the two of them didn't get back to Pryde Park until shortly before dinner.

They found Colonel Julius Raven, who had been rather crusty that morning, restored to good humour. His twinge of gout, he explained, had departed abruptly in the middle of the morning, and he had been able to go out and about upon various piscatorial occasions. These having been discharged, he now turned to what he probably regarded as the only other important duty in life – the proper exercise of hospitality. He liked to treat Appleby both as a member of the family and as a guest of some honour. There was to be a burgundy which he hoped John would just a little take notice of. If his people weren't absolute fools it ought to be breathing

46

comfortably in the dining-room now. Meantime, here was a glass of not precisely what the glorified grocers calling themselves wine-merchants were pleased to sell as a sound dry sherry nowadays.

All this was comfortable. And Appleby felt that, if he himself stood in no particular need of anything of that order, Judith did. Standing guard over Crabtree's body with a pistol in her hand had not, perhaps, especially troubled her. But the brute fact of the old man's death really had affected her. She had taken a fancy to Crabtree – or perhaps (Appleby thought) rather to the turn which that rather dubious and enigmatical person had put on. He himself had felt doubts about the fellow. And these had now been stepped up simply as a consequence of the fact that Crabtree had been murdered. Estimable people are, of course, murdered from time to time. But to be murdered is by no means to be advanced in moral rating in the regard of anybody long experienced in crime. More often than not, the lives of murderees turn out to have been far from salubrious.

Appleby sipped his sherry, and found no difficulty in having something to say about it. What did strike him as not altogether easy was the explaining to Judith's uncle that a rather nasty deed of violence had been perpetrated on the fringes of a neighbouring estate. But it was Judith who broached the matter. She did it with that sort of obliqueness which, although it would be poor form in a man, is for some reason held admissible in a woman.

'Uncle Julius,' she said, 'do you remember, long ago, an old man called Seth Crabtree?'

Colonel Raven shook his head.

'An old man called Crabtree? No, I can't say that I do. No old man called Crabtree.'

'He wouldn't have been old long ago,' Appleby interposed.

'Ah! That's another matter.' Colonel Raven's expression

47

changed. 'A damned scoundrel called Seth Crabtree, no older than myself. Yes, of course.'

'He would certainly be a contemporary of yours, more or less,' Judith agreed. 'What do you remember of him, Uncle Julius?'

'Remember of him?' Colonel Raven considered. 'Well, I can remember being minded to take a crack at the fellow's thick skull. More sherry, John?'

Quite steadily, Appleby accepted more sherry. The moment had been a startling one – the more so as a definitely alarming glint had come into Colonel Raven's usually mild eye. It was true that the Colonel's speech was, more often than not, far from an answering mildness. Knaves, fools and even damned scoundrels – if his conversation was to be trusted – were unnaturally abundant in his neighbourhood and even in his household. But this, Appleby had always supposed, was a harmless mannerism, answering to nothing in the Colonel's actual disposition towards any fellow human being. But, at the moment, the old gentleman didn't look like that.

There was a short silence, which Colonel Raven occupied by providing Judith with a second glass of sherry too. To carry on the conversation wasn't exactly easy. The announcement that somebody *had* taken a crack at Seth Crabtree's thick – or fragile – skull would have seemed, in the circumstances, a trifle bald. On the other hand, since the information had to be communicated sooner or later, to shy away from it was equally awkward.

'Crabtree is dead,' Appleby said. 'As a matter of fact, I want to tell you something about his death in a moment. But would I be right in thinking that, in his earlier years, he was a bit of a poacher?'

'A poacher!' Colonel Raven suddenly raised the decanter he was carrying in a gesture suggesting that he was about to perform some dreadful deed with it – instead of which, however, he merely studied its contents critically against the light. 'The fellow was as voracious as a pike – and a damned sight more cunning. There were times when I could have murdered him – cheerfully.'

There was again a somewhat noticeable silence.

'But' – Judith said, rather feebly – 'he went away?'

'Went away? They transported him.' Colonel Raven offered this surprising information with complete conviction.

'But, Uncle Julius, wasn't it only rather *earlier* that people were transported for poaching?'

'Was it? The more's the pity.' Colonel Raven put down the decanter, picked up a plate of small cocktail biscuits which had been set on the tray beside it, carried these over to the hearth, and there emptied them into the low fire burning in it. 'My people are all dunderheads,' he said. 'Impossible to get them out of these damned vulgar habits. Got hold of them in London hotels, I suppose. What did you say, my dear?'

'I was saying that this man Crabtree couldn't have been *transported* – sent to Botany Bay or Tasmania or somewhere. All that was stopped some time in the nineteenth century.'

'Was it?' Colonel Raven sounded faintly disappointed. 'But quite right, of course. Shockingly inhumane, and all that. Poachers, though, are another matter.'

Appleby took a moment off from this mad conversation to glance round the Colonel's library. The few engravings on the walls, and the many more engravings which he knew to be stacked away in portfolios, must represent as fine a collection of ichthyography as existed in the country. And the same went for the books. Wherever you looked, they were about fish or fishing, and nothing else. There was Badham's *Prose Halieutics* and the Marquis of Granby's *The Trout*. There was *The Papers of the Piscatorial Society*, and

49

Super Flumina and Cholmondeley Pennel's *Fishing Gossip* (which contained, Appleby remembered, that masterly discussion of 'Fishing and Fish-Hooks of the Earliest Date'). There was *Irish Salmonidae*, and General Burton's *Trouting in Norway*, and Thomas's *The Rod in India* (which suggested, Appleby thought, Kipling in one of his sadistic moods). There was Mason's *Guide to Ichthyophagy*, and there was *Bibliotheca Piscatoria*, and there was Kennedy's *Thirty Seasons in Scandinavia*. In fact there was everything. And it all added up to the proposition that Colonel Raven was very much a man of one idea. He had a mania, one might say, for the whole finny tribe.

'Anyway,' Colonel Raven was saying, 'the fellow Crabtree was packed off to the colonies.'

'Well,' Judith said, 'he went so some place in the west of the United States.'

'Precisely, my dear girl. It's what I was saying.' The Colonel appeared to meditate offering a third glass of sherry, and to think better of it. 'But why, by the way, are we talking about Crabtree? He had a job with the people over at a place called Scroop House, I seem to remember. But of course I haven't heard his name mentioned for years. Tickling other people's trout in Alaska, I should imagine.' Colonel Raven was very pleased with this joke.

'He came back.' Judith hesitated. 'He came back, only the other day. And John and I happened to meet him, and have some talk with him, in a pub called the Jolly Leggers. Only this morning, that was. And – well, he's been murdered.'

'My dear child!' Colonel Raven was shocked. 'Nothing of that sort could possibly happen round here. Just how do you suppose him to have been murdered?'

'Somebody took a crack at his skull.'

'You astound me, Judith. Who could possibly think of doing such a thing?'

'Who indeed, Uncle Julius.' Judith glanced across at Appleby almost in alarm. 'Strangely enough, it was John and I who came on the body.'

'Oh, dear!' Now Colonel Raven was really upset. He seemed at once to feel that the neighbourhood, in treating his guests to such an experience, had badly let him down. 'I'm very sorry to hear it,' he said. 'But I'm glad you mentioned it straight away. Not a subject for the dinner-table. Did I say something about the burgundy?'

'Yes, Uncle Julius. And we're looking forward to it. But I felt I had to mention what had happened, because probably the local police will be coming after John to get his help.'

'John's sort of thing, to be sure.' The Colonel had brightened again. 'I hope it's an interesting – um – case of it's kind. I'm only sorry it wasn't Stevenage.'

'Stevenage?' Judith was puzzled.

'Our local big-wig, Lord Stevenage. Murder of an earl would give John more scope, I mean. And none of us would miss old Stevenage. Not that anybody is going to miss old Crabapple, either, I suppose.'

'Crabtree.'

'Crabtree, then. They must have let him come back. Ticket-of-leave business, no doubt. Injudicious. Look at the consequences for the poor devil.'

'But, Uncle Julius, I don't think there's any reason to believe that Crabtree was a criminal.'

'A criminal?' Colonel Raven stood up as his butler announced dinner. 'You can't have heard me, my dear. The man wasn't merely a criminal. He used to take my trout.'

'And do you think he took old Mrs Coulson's trout, too?'

'Good Lord!' Colonel Raven was amused. 'I don't believe you ever met the Grand Collector when you used to come to Pryde as a kid.'

'I'm fairly sure I never even heard of her.'

'Well, well!' The Colonel made a gesture indicating that he and Judith should go in to dinner together, and that Appleby might go before or after them as he chose. 'There used to be a mixed crowd there in the old lady's day. Not our simple country set from around here at all, you know. Stevenage, for example. I don't suppose poor Tommy was ever invited to Scroop in his life. But I did occasionally go myself. The old lady liked hearing about my rather special way of tackling the *mahseer*. I'll tell you about that – just a matter, you know, of studying the way they took their ordinary feed – while we pick at whatever those dolts have provided for us.'

'We must hear that, of course, Uncle Julius. But over the coffee, please, when we can really attend. At dinner you must tell us about old Mrs Coulson and her mixed crowd. I feel cheated at never having heard all about her before.'

'It's no good,' Appleby said over Colonel Raven's shoulder. 'Judith isn't being honest. She wants people, and the local legends, and what sort of *chinoiseries* William Chambers did for the original Coulson – if that was his name. She prefers that – and let's be frank about it – to anything about fish.'

'It isn't true,' Judith said. 'But I can't deny that it is really John who has a passion for the fishy. Anything of that sort he pounces on at once.'

'To be sure, my dear.' Colonel Raven answered a shade absently. Arrived in his dining-room, he was giving a sharp eye to the dispositions that the dolts had contrived for his guests. 'But I can certainly tell you about the folk at Scroop. The house is one of those new-fangled places that retired merchants and their kind began running up in the 1770s and 1780s. But people of that sort have their merits, one oughtn't to deny. As for old Sara Coulson I'll tell you all I know.'

Chapter Five

'Reasonable family, and all that,' Colonel Raven presently said, as he peered with some severity at a sauceboat. 'Daughter of old Freddie Crispin, who was the brainiest of that lot.'

'The Viceroy?' Appleby asked.

'That's the chap. Shot with him once, when I was a lad. Rather a set affair. Had to perch on a great elephant, and all that. But quite fun. Unassuming for a big-wig. Freddie, I mean. Not the elephant.'

'So old Mrs Coulson,' Judith said, 'was an Hon? I'm surprised Seth Crabtree didn't make that point.'

'Yes, of course. She was the Honourable Mrs Coulson, for what the point's worth. But rather distinguished, bless her, as well. All sorts of people congregated. Arthur Balfour, and that crowd. Sara might have been called a tuft-hunter, if she hadn't been quite a tuft herself. But mad – quite mad. Do you know, mad folk have always interested me? Something that rather appeals in them. I don't know what.'

'And she was called the Grand Collector?'

'So she was. And so she did. Religions and reptiles, pottery and prima donnas, ormolu and O.M.s.' Colonel Raven smiled happily – whether at his own wit or because the sauce was right, it would have been hard to say.

'I'm sure Arthur Balfour had the O.M. And was well up in a variety of religions as well.'

'Not a doubt of it, my dear – all credit to him. Always found one religion a pretty full ration, myself. Keeping up with it, and all that. And going in and reading one of the lessons for the parson. Morning on your knees in the family pew – and knowing, perhaps, that the mayfly are on the water. Hard.'

'Yes, Uncle Julius. But tell us more about Sara Coulson.'

'Some money of her own. And then, of course, this fellow Coulson had pots. It always helps.'

'She survived her husband?'

'Dear me, yes. By a good many years. And was left the place absolutely. No entail, or trust, or anything of that sort. No children, you see – and next-of-kin Coulsons only out on rather a remote line.'

'But there's a Coulson at Scroop House now?'

'Certainly. A very nice chap. Always anxious to do the right thing in the county. Too anxious, in a way. Place not quite native to him.'

'I see. But how did he come there?'

'Bless me if I ever thought to inquire. Never been on more than nodding terms with Scroop, you see. But I suppose the old lady must have made a will handing it back to the Coulson who was next in succession. Her own fortune too, perhaps – since she was certainly anxious that the place should be kept up in the grand manner.'

'And the new Coulson let her down there?'

'It seems to me you know all about this story already.' The Colonel frowned in some displeasure. But this may have been only because his butler was showing signs of handling the burgundy as only a dolt would do.

'The late Seth Crabtree,' Appleby explained, 'gave us a glimpse of life in the big house long ago. He seems to have had some position of privilege with the old lady. Did something or other for her. It was all a little obscure.'

'Perhaps he provided her kitchens with my trout. He'd have been quite capable of it, the atrocious rascal. But – by Jove! – I've remembered something. About this very decent

54

fellow, Bertram Coulson, coming into the place. People were surprised at it. You see, although he was the nearest of kin, old Sara had never set eyes on him. And there was some other Coulson – a younger man – whom she was said to have rather a fancy for. And the house and money were, as I've said, hers to do what she liked with. So people thought it odd. And it's odd that this should come back to me. The story hasn't been in my head for years. But then, so many things haven't.' Colonel Raven, who was sniffing warily at a drop of burgundy, looked momentarily perplexed. 'I'm sure I don't know why.'

'But about when old Mrs Coulson died?' Judith prompted. 'Bertram Coulson failed to take over?'

'Oh, entirely. Never so much as came to look at the place at that time. Shoved it on the market as a furnished property, with shooting, fishing and all, with the result that it was rented by a commercial chap called Binns. Later on, when Bertram Coulson thought better of it and came into residence after all, his former conduct took some living down in the neighbourhood.'

'How did his change of heart come about?'

'I don't know at all, my dear. But it was deuced sudden. Perhaps it would never have happened, but for the bust-up in the Binns *ménage*. Mrs Binns cleared out. Indeed, as she cleared out, they say, without so much as paying her milliner, she may be said to have levanted. Immoral woman, as a matter of fact.'

'I see. She went off with another man?'

'I suppose so. But, as far as I know, nobody ever saw her or heard of her again. Unusual, come to think of it, among the propertied classes. But, no doubt, there were lawyers in on settling the affair, and they got their whack.'

'And then the commercial Mr Binns quit too?'

'Very suddenly, my dear. And that's where the queer

part of the story comes. Binns and Bertram Coulson had some sort of business connexion. In fact, one gathered that they were quite pals. The arrangement for Binns's tenancy, in consequence, had become rather casual. The current lease hadn't been renewed up to within a few weeks, or days, of its being due to expire. Then there was this scandal about Mrs Binns. And Bertram Coulson had a belated fit of conscience about Scroop and what it should stand for. So he came down and virtually turfed Binns out on the spot. The story is that his books arrived in one van, his linen in another and his sporting gear in a third. And there he was: a Coulson at Scroop once more. Later on, he must have made it up with Binns. I've never heard, indeed, that Binns has been back to the place himself. But he has a couple of children who stay with the Coulsons quite often. Grown up now. Lad called Peter, and girl of the name of Daphne.'

'So there's a Mrs Coulson?' Judith asked.

'Certainly. And a devilish fine woman, in a mature way. No children, though. I see her from time to time. Her body speaks, if you ask me.'

Appleby, who had been listening attentively, was startled.

'What was that?' he asked.

'Shakespeare.' Colonel Raven produced one of his rare contented smiles as he made this unexpected reply. 'Cleopatra, would it be? No harm in frankness with a married woman, my dear.' And the Colonel gave an ingenuously conspiratorial nod to Judith. 'Idle and childless women of a certain age. They sometimes develop a roving eye.' The Colonel hesitated. 'And turn up in unexpected places.'

'In fact' – Judith interpreted – 'Mrs Bertram Coulson is no better than Mrs Binns was?'

This time the Colonel shook his head.

'No, no,' he said hastily. 'One mustn't say that. Dashed

56

serious thing to say. No evidence, at all. Or very little. But flighty – yes.'

Appleby watched, with considerable satisfaction, more burgundy being poured into his glass. Only Colonel Raven's butler was now in attendance. As well as being a dolt, Appleby reflected, he must be a decidedly confidential servant.

'You said one thing, Colonel, about the belated arrival of Bertram Coulson that struck me. Clearly the man would need some personal possessions, including his own collection of books, and so on. But why sporting gear? He'd apparently ignored, for years and years, being the possessor of a large sporting property. I don't get a picture of the fellow at all.'

Colonel Raven considered this for a moment. He took a sip of burgundy and considered it again.

'The man's a romantic idealist,' he said.

Both the Applebys had found this so surprising an expression to drop from Uncle Julius that a moment's silence succeeded. Appleby caught the butler's eye, and had a feeling that it had turned more than commonly inexpressive. But, oddly enough, it was to his butler that Colonel Raven now turned.

'Tarbox,' he said, 'you would agree with me?'

'Yes, sir – although I am not quite clear on the score of the qualificatory epithet. "Romantic", sir, I confess to be obscure to me. But "idealist", certainly. Only a very considerable idealist would have considered retaining the services of the man Hollywood.'

'Hollywood, Tarbox?'

'Mr Coulson's butler, sir. He had been many years at Scroop House, and served both Mr Binns and the Honourable Mrs Coulson before him. But to my mind, sir, he is a person to be deprecated.'

'Deprecated, Tarbox?'

'"To advise the avoidance of" is, I understand, sir, the common signification of the term. I should advise the avoidance of the person under review.'

'Dash it all, Tarbox, this Hollywood isn't under review, and I certainly have no intention of looking him up. And now I have quite forgotten what *is* under review, as you call it.'

'The temperamental characteristics of Mr Coulson, sir. You were remarking that he is a romantic idealist. Her ladyship will correct me if I have repeated the expression incorrectly.'

'It was certainly the Colonel's phrase,' Judith said.

'Thank you, my lady.' Tarbox bowed gravely and withdrew – apparently upon some mission connected with the service of dessert.

'The dolt's no fool,' Colonel Raven said. 'He agrees with me – although he was determined to confuse the issue with rubbishing talk about somebody called I've already forgotten what. But at least you're now clear about Bertram Coulson.'

Appleby shook his head, laughing.

'Not in the least,' he said. 'But was it his romantic idealism that prevented him from coming to live at Scroop when he first inherited it?'

'Yes – I think it was.' Colonel Raven sounded at once convinced and a trifle vague, as if an unwonted clarity of perception were now failing him. 'That sort of thing – yes.'

'You mean that he felt he couldn't live up to the place? Then why did he shove in this Binns, who doesn't sound to have been much of a catch?'

'Perhaps he was taken in by him.' Colonel Raven made another big effort. 'Bertram Coulson wouldn't *quite* notice, you see, if a fellow was a bit of a phoney.' The Colonel paused, and looked anxiously at his niece. 'Would that be the expression, my dear? I had it from Tarbox, as a matter of fact.'

'Quite right, Uncle Julius. And is the reason that Bertram Coulson wouldn't quite notice if a fellow was a bit of a phoney really that he's a bit of a phoney himself?'

'I wouldn't care to put it that way. He's not at all a bad chap, as I said. But you couldn't call him an easy man. Might have something in his past, you know. Or that inferiority business the psychologists talk about. Sometimes, I've thought him rather like an actor feeling his way into a what's-it-called.'

'A role?'

'Just that, my dear. I expect those books were all about how to be an English landed gentleman, and that the sporting gear was all stuff he'd gathered from them he ought to possess.'

'He doesn't sound a very sterling character, Uncle Julius.'

'But that's just what I don't want to say. Or at least what I don't *know*.' Colonel Raven sounded almost distressed. 'He's not unattractive. He has a kind of innocent joy in feeling that he's begun to know the ropes.'

'Did he come, then,' Judith asked, 'from so very unpolished or unsophisticated an environment?'

'I believe he owned sheep or cattle in rather a big way in Australia. I've talked to him about the place, as a matter of fact. It seems that they have trout and they have fish. What isn't a trout is a fish. Obviously an undeveloped place.'

'But, Uncle Julius, people who own sheep in rather a big way in Australian pastoral country could most of them step into the proprietorship of an English estate entirely in their stride.'

'That may be, my dear. But it's my view of Bertram Coulson that he has some sort of' – Colonel Raven searched the air – 'some sort of thingummy built into him.'

'Diffidence?'

'That's the word. Mind you, he isn't retiring. He's eager to be on his game, and all that. But he has some picture of himself that he can't feel certain he's living up to. Tarbox' – and the Colonel turned in appeal to his butler, who had returned to the dining-room accompanied by an alarmed assistant of tender years for the purpose of removing the table-cloth – 'Tarbox, what am I talking about?'

'I believe the term to be *persona*, sir.'

'That's it.'

'But there are other expressions. "Ego-ideal" might also be applicable.' Tarbox turned to Appleby. 'I think, sir,' he murmured, 'that you will elect to stay with the burgundy?'

Appleby did elect to stay with the burgundy. He watched Colonel Raven moving to port and Judith to Sauternes. Tarbox, he reflected, was more than a mere philologist.

'What about Binns, the late tenant?' he asked the Colonel. 'Did you form any impression of him? But perhaps you didn't much run into him.'

'Oh, dear me, yes.' Colonel Raven spoke almost severely. 'You must take one fellow with another, you know. And there was a lot that was sound about Alfred Binns. Particularly on the Caribbean. He'd fished some pretty monsters out of it. He used to drop in for a yarn. And he gave me a book to add to my collection. Rather well written thing. Called *The Old Man and the Sea*.'

'But you haven't seen him lately?'

'Lord, no. Not for quite a number of years. His kids stay at Scroop, as I said. But I don't suppose Binns himself ever comes near this part of the world now.'

'On the contrary, sir.'

This was a murmur from Tarbox, and Colonel Raven turned to him in surprise.

'What's that, Tarbox?'

'Mr Binns is now in the library, sir. He has called. The hour being a trifle on the early side for an after-dinner visit, I thought it well to accommodate him there.'

'Well, I'm blessed!'

'I have provided whisky, sir. But with some shade of hesitation.'

'Like that, is it?'

'Yes, sir. And her ladyship will find coffee in the drawing-room.'

'The deuce she will!'

'Yes, sir. I judged it possible she might not wish to join the gentlemen until the conclusion of Mr Binns's visit.'

'I see. Is the fellow bad?'

'Why, no, sir. Only a trifle heavy. *Vino gravis*, as it was expressed by the ancients.'

'Blockhead means a bit lit up,' Colonel Raven explained, when Tarbox had withdrawn again. He was clearly impressed by this latest exhibition of his butler's linguistic knowledge. 'Alfred Binns always was a little that way. But no vice in him, you know.'

'I'm touched,' Judith said, 'by Tarbox's anxiety to preserve me from anything unedifying. But I take it that Mr Binns isn't violent in his cups?'

'Lord, no, my dear. The man wouldn't hurt a fly.'

It wasn't at all clear to Appleby – when he had been introduced to Alfred Binns some ten minutes later – that the former tenant of Scroop House was in fact drunk. Tarbox, he was disposed to feel, had keener philological than physiological perception. It was true that Binns had been drinking, since he did faintly smell of whisky. But he had the appearance – at least to an expert eye – of a man suffering from the effect of shock rather than of a man suffering from the effect of alcohol.

'Delighted to see you after all these years,' Colonel Raven was saying amiably. 'Hope you have time to stop and have a bit of a yarn, my dear Binns. Conditions have changed over there a good deal, I've been told.'

'Changed, have they?' Binns was a heavily built man in his middle fifties. He possessed, Appleby felt, that kind of powerful personality which makes it difficult to take a guess at some men's antecedents and background. Binns might have come a long way – and done so by exercising a good deal of ruthlessness *en route*. He was a man who could make stiff, quick decisions and stick to them. On the other hand, there was some obscure point at which he was vulnerable. And it was possible to feel that, quite lately, this point had been touched.

'Decidedly changed,' Colonel Raven went on. 'No time ago at all, I heard of a fellow getting drowned – and in a deuced queer way.'

'I know nothing of that.' It was with some abruptness that Binns offered this reply.

'Ah, you must be a bit out of touch. Shooting, too.'

'Shooting?' Binns glanced rapidly from Colonel Raven to Appleby and back again. 'Shooting at Scroop?'

Colonel Raven stared.

'Scroop, my dear fellow? They don't have lobsters at Scroop.'

'*Lobsters?*' Alfred Binns had flushed darkly, as if suspecting he was being made a fool of.

'Drowned while up to something called skin diving, my dear Binns. And stalking lobsters and shooting them under water. Big fish too, in the same way. Stalk them across the ocean bed with some sort of electric gun. Would *you* call that angling, now? It's a nice point.'

'Good heavens, Raven – what on earth are you talking about?'

62

'Sea, my dear chap, not earth. And the Caribbean, of course. Great changes since the days we used to talk about.'

Appleby, who found these absurd cross-purposes sufficiently entertaining, wondered whether they might not conceivably be instructive as well.

'Do you often,' he asked, 'revisit your old haunts in this part of the country?'

'No – and it's not what I'm doing now.' Binns again spoke with a shade more abruptness than was to be expected in one making a social call. At the same time he gave Appleby a sharp considering glance. It was evident that he hadn't at all placed Colonel Raven's guest. 'Driving rather rapidly through,' he went on. 'But I didn't feel I should simply pass the Colonel by.'

'Quite right, Binns. I take it very kindly in you.' The Colonel was all hospitality. 'But have you dined, my dear fellow? My donkeys can dish you up a meal of sorts in a jiffy.'

'Thank you. But I had dinner fifty miles away. And how is the great work going forward, Raven?'

This very proper inquiry about the *Atlas and Entomology of the Dry-Fly Streams of England* was made by Binns with every appearance of interest and cordiality, and it set the Colonel talking at once. Appleby sat back and listened. And it was presently clear to him that Alfred Binns, whatever might have been his past activities in the Caribbean, retained very little genuine piscatory concern. Moreover he continued to suggest a man in some way obscurely perturbed. Unless – Appleby thought – he had turned in to Pryde Park on a momentary impulse which he was now regretting, and unless he was simply preoccupied with some entirely extraneous business or personal concern, it looked as if some ulterior purpose in his visit must soon discover itself. He was drinking a stiff whisky, and no doubt he had drunk an earlier one while the Colonel and the Applebys were finishing dinner. But Tarbox's diagnosis remained a faulty one. Any fair-minded police surgeon would have judged Binns sober.

'And how are your children?' Colonel Raven asked. 'Not that "children" is at all the proper word for them now, I suppose.'

'Peter and Daphne?' Binns, who had been feigning interest in the Colonel's fish, now seemed to Appleby to be equally feigning absence of interest in his own progeny. 'What do I ever know of Peter and Daphne? They roam about, you know. I can't get Peter interested in the business – and as for Daphne, I can't even get her interested in a young man. Seen anything of them lately, yourself? Or heard anything?'

For a moment Colonel Raven was surprised. Then he remembered.

'But of course. They stay at Scroop from time to time. I was mentioning it to Appleby. But, if either of them is there now, I haven't heard of it. I doubt whether I should. They mightn't look in on me, as you have so very decently done, my dear chap.'

Binns nodded absently, as one dismissing the most casual of subjects.

'I had an idea,' he said, 'of looking up Bertram Coulson as well. We were very good friends at one time. There was a little awkwardness when he ended my tenancy so abruptly, but that belongs to the past. I'm glad my children keep up a link. How does he get along?'

'Coulson? Well enough, I think. I was giving Appleby a fair account of him as a good neighbour earlier this evening. But we don't run into each other a great deal.'

Binns nodded – again absently, as if this too were a matter only of casual interest. Then he rose.

'I must be getting along,' he said. 'And a call on Bertram must keep for another time. I've still got a hundred miles to put on the clock. Just shooting through, as I said.'

'But can't I persuade you to stay the night?' Colonel Raven was hospitably distressed. 'Absolutely delighted if you could.'

Binns shook his head. And the gesture, although accompanied by expressions which were sufficiently polite, gave Appleby the impression of a man who was now regretting some futile act. The three men moved to the door of the library. Appleby took a deft sideways step, which brought Binns full-face before him.

'What do you think,' he asked, 'about Crabtree's death?'

There was a moment's silence which might, or might not, have been of incomprehension merely.

'I beg your pardon?' Binns spoke to an effect of rather more courtesy than was native to him.

'Seth Crabtree.' And Appleby looked straight at Binns. 'He has been killed. Today. Did you know?'

'My dear sir, I don't even know what you are talking about.' Binns seemed about to break off this exchange and take his leave. Then he gave a start of surprise. 'Did you say Crabtree? When I had Scroop, there was a fellow of that name working about the place. But he went abroad. You don't mean him?'

'I do. He was found dead this afternoon, and the facts point to foul play.'

'I'm sorry to hear it, I'm sure. But of course I have heard nothing of it. As I explained, I'm simply driving rapidly through.'

'So that early this afternoon you were, in fact, nowhere near this part of the world?'

'I was a long way off, Sir John, and with no notion of the impertinent curiosity I might be running into. Good

T – A.C.C. – C

night.' And Alfred Binns gave a curt nod and strode into the hall, where Colonel Raven was waiting for him.

For a minute Appleby remained where he was. Binns, he was thinking, had some claim to be called formidable. He had been a man for some reason thrown off his balance at the start of his odd call. But he had met that sudden sharp attack like a rock.

The Colonel was bidding his guest farewell outside his front door. Appleby slipped through the hall and into the drawing-room. Judith was rather impatiently turning over a copy of *The Field*.

'Well,' she said challengingly, 'was Mr Binns really unfit for mixed company?'

'Absolutely not.' As he spoke, Appleby flicked off the lights, walked over to a window, and drew back a curtain.

Outside, there was summer darkness. But to the left, from the main portico of Pryde Park, a glow of electric light fell across the drive.

'Listen,' Appleby said. 'A nice noise – wouldn't you say? Or hardly a noise at all.'

'What on earth – '

'And now look.'

'Well, well.' Judith, having looked, said no more. So there was no sound except the gentle purr of the silver-grey Rolls-Royce which had circled before them and was now departing into the night.

Chapter Six

There was nothing out of the way in Appleby's sitting up in the library at Pryde to smoke a final solitary pipe, and it was thus that Tarbox found him.

'Is there anything further that you will require, sir?'

'Thank you, Tarbox, nothing at all. The only thing that I could do with is a little light on this afternoon's bad business.'

'Yes, indeed, sir. It was a most distressing incident for her ladyship to become involved in. But I fear I cannot assist you to any solution. An enigmatical catastrophe, sir.'

'Do you yourself remember anything of this old fellow, Seth Crabtree, back in Mrs Coulson's time, or during the years he remained at Scroop after Mr Binns had taken over?'

'Neither of these periods may be described as of yesterday, sir. But I think I may claim to be not without a modicum of reminiscence.'

'Would you describe Crabtree as having been some sort of confidant of Mrs Coulson's?'

'Yes. I believe, that is to say, that there was some such impression abroad, sir. A confidant in humble station, of course. Crabtree could never have been categorized as an upper servant. He remained an outdoor man.'

Appleby nodded.

'Yes, he told me as much himself. Have you any idea of just what may have recommended him to the old lady?'

'None whatever, sir, I am sorry to say. Of course he was a great one with the ladies.'

'Old Crabtree was a great one with the ladies!' Appleby stared. 'You surprise me very much.'

'You must not let it escape your recollection, sir, that Crabtree was scarcely old Crabtree at that time – neither during Mrs Coulson's life nor when Mr Binns began his tenancy of Scroop. He was middle-aged, of course. But men of the world, sir, are cognizant – are they not? – of the powerful attraction which some males exercise over the fair sex at that period of life.' Tarbox paused. 'Favoured males,' he added, a shade unexpectedly.

'Yes, to be sure. But you don't suggest that Mrs Coulson – ?'

'Certainly not, sir. *Honi soit qui mal y pense*, if the old adage may be allowed me. Mrs Coulson, although highly eccentric, was even more highly virtuous.'

'She was eccentric?' Appleby jumped at this. 'Not merely as having a passion for knowing great people, and that sort of thing?'

'No, sir. That, if I may venture the thought, is somewhat too widely diffused a foible to be felicitously subsumed within the concept of eccentricity. Mrs Coulson was otherwise odd.'

'I see. But just how otherwise?'

'I am afraid I cannot help you to further definition, sir. It was common averment, no more. And I was not myself much in the habit of frequenting the society at Scroop. An occasional cup of tea in the housekeeper's room – yes. But any confabulation with the man Hollywood in the butler's pantry – no.'

'Ah, yes – Hollywood.' Appleby had got to his feet and was leaning against the chimney-piece. It seemed a more companionable way of continuing what Tarbox would have called this colloquy. 'You don't care for Hollywood?'

'Well, sir, there is the name, to begin with. I confess to a certain sensitiveness in the matter of nomenclature. And "Hollywood", to my mind, is a name in the highest degree absurd.'

'I don't quite chime in about the degree, Tarbox. But I give it to you that it's a silly name. Have you no other reason for objecting to the butler over there?'

For the first time, Tarbox hesitated. A butler – Appleby felt – is a butler, after all. And it is not lightly that one denounces one of one's peers.

'One must be allowed one's intuitive responses, sir.' Suddenly Tarbox hesitated no longer. 'No villainy would surprise me in the man Hollywood. A veritable Tarquin, that man might be.'

'Good heavens!' Appleby was properly startled by this. 'But Crabtree would have no need to be a Tarquin?'

'Very true, sir. Crabtree had a way with him, as I ventured to intimate. Even with the ladies, it may be. And certainly with the – um – wenches.'

'I see.' This eighteenth-century species of discrimination again properly impressed Appleby.

'It was observed by an eminent historian, sir, that absolute power corrupts absolutely. And it is not so very long ago that the butler in a great establishment – or at least a *large* establishment, since we must not exaggerate the consequence of Scroop House – was in something like that position in regard to a number of young persons.'

'What you have to tell me interests me very much.' As he said this, Appleby found himself wondering whether the respectable and polysyllabic Tarbox was the victim of some sexual obsession. The unknown Hollywood might well be a Tarquin, but the conception of the late Seth Crabtree as a Don Juan was a difficult one. Yet it might be perfectly valid. Appleby retained a vivid impression of how he had himself found Crabtree a puzzling character. Judith hadn't agreed; she had accepted him as a sensitive and simple old person, much attached to ancient ways and days. Perhaps she was right. And Crabtree could never offer any further explanation of himself now.

But Crabtree wasn't the only dubious character Appleby had heard of in connexion with Scroop House. The present Mrs Coulson, Bertram Coulson's wife, was flighty. Her predecessor as mistress of the place, Mrs Binns, who had cleared out, was roundly described by Colonel Raven as an immoral woman. And Bertram Coulson himself sounded distinctly odd.

'It might be useful,' Appleby said, 'to know a little more of the actual circumstances under which Crabtree left England. When I talked to him – and my wife and I, you know, had quite a lot of conversation with him almost immediately before his death – he gave me the impression that it was simply a matter of his not liking the way things were going at Scroop. The Binns régime offended him. He hung on for a time, and then he quit. But for how long a time? I haven't got a grip on any kind of time scheme yet. Can you help me there? Although it's a shame to keep you up any longer.'

'Not at all, sir. I appreciate that, in giving you any intelligence that I can, I am in a manner of speaking assisting the operation of the law. Moreover, sir, I have a particular occasion tonight for not retiring at an early hour. As to the matter of the chronological disposition of events, I believe I can be of some assistance to you. Old Mrs Coulson died in 1940, and Mr Binns – Mr Bertram Coulson's tenant, as you know – moved in almost at once. The celerity of the operation was remarked upon.'

'And Mr Binns already had a family?'

'Only a son, Master Peter Binns, at that time. He would have been about five years old. The daughter, Miss Daphne, was born at the end of the following year. 1941, that is to say.'

'And the scandalous departure of Mrs Binns?'

'That cannot have been until 1950. As the Colonel, I believe, apprised you, it was an event immediately followed by the ending of Mr Binns's tenancy and Mr Bertram Coulson's coming into residence.'

'So that takes us to a date about ten years back – and old Mrs Coulson's death occurred ten years before that again.'

'Precisely so, sir. And memory can be faulty at such an interval. But I believe that such information as I have given you is tolerably accurate.'

'I'm most grateful.' Appleby reflected for a moment. 'We've been talking mostly about Scroop House and its occupants – usefully, no doubt, since Crabtree was employed there. But there must have been another aspect to his life, after all. The village and the village people, and so forth. What were Crabtree's relations with them? Did he have a family in the village? Did his leaving it to go overseas raise any talk at the time? There's a good deal of that sort of thing to be found out.'

'Clearly so, sir. But I fear I can be of no help to you. We have our own village here – and I confess that I find one enough for me. But both Upper and Nether Scroop will have their gossip, one may safely suppose.'

'I think Upper Scroop is close to the house?'

'Yes, sir. And Nether Scroop is no more than a hamlet, a little south of the canal where it enters the tunnel.'

'Ah, yes – I've been there. Or at least I've been to the Jolly Leggers. By the way, do you happen to know the publican there? Manager, he would probably call himself.'

'I know him only by name, sir. Channing-Kennedy, I think. Obviously a socially anomalous person. It is my experience that they are best avoided.'

Appleby laughed.

'I think my wife would agree with you. She didn't take to Channing-Kennedy at all. And now I think we'd both better go to bed. But I'll just finish this pipe.'

'Thank you, sir. You will no doubt extinguish the light.'

And Tarbox glanced round the room, spotted an ash-tray with a couple of match-sticks in it, picked this up with ceremonial gravity, bowed, and withdrew.

Appleby lingered no more than five minutes. He had a suspicion that the Crabtree affair might yet cost him a sleepless night or two. As yet, however, he lacked sufficient information to render vigil profitable. Fortunately he was not obsessed by it. He would be asleep within the next ten minutes.

But this programme failed to fulfil itself. Appleby, obedient to Tarbox's injunction, turned off the lights in the library before stepping into the hall. Here there was only a single low light at the far end. Not quite seeing where he was going, he only just saved himself from colliding with somebody who had been hurrying past the door.

'I beg your pardon.' Appleby stepped back as he apologized. At the same moment, he remembered a light-switch close to his hand, and decided that the situation would be clarified if he depressed it. And this proved to be the case. The person into whose arms he had almost tumbled was the man who had hurried past Judith and himself on the towpath.

'I can't think where Tarbox – ' The stranger broke off as he recognized Appleby. Then he instantly carried on with what he had been proposing to say. ' – has taken himself off to. Still, I've seen myself off these premises often enough.' He gave Appleby a smile that was formal rather than cordial. 'No doubt, sir, you are a guest of Colonel Raven's. And perhaps I ought to explain, if Tarbox doesn't turn up to vindicate me – that I am not to be regarded as a suspicious character. My name is West, and I am the local doctor. Tarbox summoned me on an emergency call – and quite right he proves to have been.'

'But nothing really serious, I hope?' Appleby asked.

West produced another bleak smile.

'That must be said to depend on how seriously you take the pleasures of the table. For I'm afraid the Colonel's cook must have her appendix out in rather a hurry. So excuse me, please. I was making my way to the telephone.'

Appleby stepped back, and Dr West passed him with a nod. There seemed no harm in waiting until he had called an ambulance or accomplished whatever else he was about. Indeed, as Tarbox was still invisible, it seemed the civil course. And presently the doctor came back.

'No danger for an hour or two,' he said. 'And she'll be in the surgeon's hands by then.' He gave a quick glance round the hall, as if looking for his hat or coat.

'I think,' Appleby said, 'that we've met – or rather encountered each other – earlier today?'

There was a moment's silence, during which Appleby was visited by the odd conviction that West was meditating denying this blankly. As it was, the man seemed to temporize.

'Indeed?' he said interrogatively.

'And my wife was with me at the time. We speculated – you will forgive me – as to whether you might not be the local G.P.'

'Ah, yes – on the towpath.' West said this indifferently. 'I often take a walk that way.'

'Do you, indeed?' Appleby was equally indifferent. 'It seemed to us that very few people do. We may be described as having met in an isolated situation.'

'Indeed?' West looked coolly at Appleby. 'This part of the country is familiar to you?'

'Far from it. Although my wife, who is Colonel Raven's niece, has been here from time to time. My name, by the way, is Appleby.'

'Ah, yes – Sir John Appleby.' West made no great ado about this. 'I was going to say that, to strangers, appearances may be deceptive. There may have been more people around this afternoon than you think.'

'That may well be so.'

'Sir John, may I ask' – and again West produced the bleak smile – 'whether you are proposing to take a professional interest in the affair that our conversation appears to be veering towards?'

A cool card, this – Appleby thought. Aloud, he said:

'I see you have heard about Crabtree?'

'Crabtree?' West shook his head. 'I don't know the name. But I've heard that, hard by where we passed each other, some unfortunate man has been hit on the head. I'm not the police surgeon, as you may know, so I've heard no more than that. But it's an unusual sort of thing in these parts. In no time, I think' – and again there came the bleak smile – 'we shall all be suspecting each other of all sorts of crimes.'

'No doubt we shall.'

'And, Sir John – oddly enough – the general opinion will be that any strangers in the neighbourhood will be the first who ought to give an account of themselves.'

'Will it, indeed.' Appleby judged this last remark of West's impertinent. But he gave no sign of this. 'Crabtree,' he said, 'was a villager here who went overseas about fifteen years ago, and had apparently only just come back. Perhaps your own acquaintance with the district is of more recent date?'

'Decidedly. I came from quite another part of the country to take over the practice here only three years ago.'

'Ah. Then I'm afraid, Dr West, that you may get missed out in the general epidemic of suspicions you have been predicting. Crabtree, you see, can have had only a few hours in which to get seriously across anybody for the first time here. So unless we are to imagine that he had been followed to this part of the world by somebody with whom he had developed bad relations fairly recently, we seem obliged to view his murder – for murder it certainly was – as a matter of the settling of some very old score indeed.'

'I can see some force in that train of reasoning.' West spoke as a man who doesn't, in fact, think any too highly of the proposition being put to him. 'But one can surely imagine a motive generating itself, so to speak, more or less on the spot. Robbery, for example.'

'Yes, that is true. But there is no sign that this unfortunate fellow had much to be robbed of.'

'He had returned, you say, from foreign parts. He might have had savings – and, if so, they were probably on his person. Even if his appearance was shabby, as you seem to suggest, that might hold. And he may have been observed fingering them over. Or he may have confided rashly in some stranger, or former acquaintance. Isn't robbery the commonest motive in the category of crime you appear to be dealing with?'

'Probably it is.' Appleby was reflecting that this was, at least, a clear-headed man. At the same time he was remembering the curious impression that West had made upon him on the occasion of his brushing past on the towpath. 'Crabtree had a few shillings in his pocket, no more. And nothing to give any line on his recent movements.'

'A few shillings?' Dr West had found his hat, and seemed about to show himself out into the night. The interest he was taking in the death of Crabtree, if intelligent, was very far from being absorbed. 'Doesn't that suggest robbery? He may have returned to England far from prosperous. But he would scarcely be destitute.'

'That is true. But a criminal of any astuteness, having killed Crabtree upon some motive other than that of immediate financial gain, would be likely to take his wallet, pocket-book or whatever before throwing the body into the lock. It would set the police on a false trail.'

'No doubt.' West's attitude was again approaching indifference as he moved towards the front door.

'As a matter of fact, there is one suggestion of robbery in the affair. Crabtree was in possession of something when I myself encountered him at the Jolly Leggers that had disappeared when we found the body. But it was of no conceivable value.'

'Is that so?' West's hand was on the door. 'You'll forgive me if I get off to bed. On my job, one has to go rather short of sleep from time to time.'

'I'd hate to cause you a single sleepless hour, Dr West. Good night.'

Chapter Seven

On the following morning the Applebys went walking again. This time their objective was avowedly Scroop House. Colonel Raven had rung up Bertram Coulson and announced the proposed call. That the Crabtree affair was, so to speak, in its hinterland had been left as well-understood.

'Do you think it may have been Uncle Julius?' Judith asked, as they walked down the drive. She put the question with a great air of comfortable chat.

'It's no doubt a possibility that should be inquired into,' Appleby said a trifle shortly. 'And Tarbox. And the cook. She must be severely questioned as soon as they've had her appendix out. And, for that matter, the whole blessed neighbourhood. The vicar. The vet. The district nurse. The delightful fellow who was anxious to deliver a piano. And Channing-Kennedy, who refused to have one.'

'Channing-Kennedy?' Judith seemed to take this last suggestion seriously and almost hopefully. She must really have taken a most particular dislike to the landlord of the Jolly Leggers. 'But surely Channing-Kennedy almost has an alibi provided by ourselves?'

'I think not. A bicycle along that secondary road, south of the canal, would have done the trick. The road, incidentally, which was being graced by the progress of Mr Alfred Binns's Phantom V at an hour when Mr Binns would like it to be believed that he was a couple of counties away. There's not going to be any shortage of suspects in this business. So you needn't begin by talking nonsense about your uncle.'

'It isn't nonsense.' With some surprise, Appleby saw that

Judith was speaking seriously now. 'You know that all my family are mad.'

'That's perfectly true – in a popular manner of speaking. My own experience of Ravens includes one or two bizarre episodes, I must confess.'

'Very well. And at least part of what Uncle Julius had to say about Seth Crabtree last night was pretty mad, wasn't it? All that about poaching.'

'It certainly doesn't quite knit with your uncle's generally amiable character. He talks about poachers and so on rather like an eighteenth-century comic squire in a novel. But I take it to be some sort of private joke or affectation, like his calling all those old servants he doats on dunderheads and rascals.'

'He did get out and about yesterday, although he wasn't expected to. Suppose he met Crabtree by the lock, recognized him, said something like "You damned scoundrel!" and gave him a whack on the head. What then?'

'What then?' Appleby considered this fantastic-seeming question soberly. 'Well, your uncle would have walked back to Pryde and said something like "Tarbox, I've taken a crack at an atrocious ruffian and knocked him into the canal. He's probably dead."' Appleby glanced at Judith. 'Wouldn't something like that be the way of it?'

'I don't know.'

'Dash it all, girl, you can't imagine your uncle embarking on an elaborate course of deceit, can you? We're not in a whodunnit, you know, with everybody capable of anything.'

'But, John, Uncle Julius *is* rather mad. And don't mad people do things and then just forget about them?'

'A good many crimes of violence, impulsive in nature, are only imperfectly preserved in the conscious memories of those who commit them. But it takes a rare and absolute mania blankly to lose all recollection of such a thing. If we had dinner last night in the company of a homicidal maniac, we shall make quite a name for ourselves, believe me, in the annals of psychiatry. Hullo, here's the lock again.'

'Yes,' Judith said. 'And some morbid persons peering at it.'

The police had concluded such investigations of the spot as they judged might be useful, and there was now no trace of what had happened there. The gates on the down-falling side were open, as Appleby and Judith had managed to drag them. The other gates were, of course, closed, and a young man and woman were standing on them, staring gloomily at the water.

'Not villagers,' Judith said. 'Hikers? Not that, either. There aren't any young Coulsons, are there?'

'I gather not. And my guess is that these are the young Binnses, who stay with the Coulsons from time to time. You know, I had several ideas about the call of Binns *père* at Pryde last night. And one of them was that he came fishing for information as to the whereabouts of his progeny.'

'He can't be very trustful of them.'

'At the moment, the young people don't look very trustful of each other.'

This was true. The girl and youth on the gates did now seem to be in attitudes suggesting that they were at odds with one another. At this moment, however, they became aware of the Applebys. And it was possible to feel them as joining forces immediately.

'Good morning,' Appleby said, when he had come up with them. 'Am I right in thinking that, if we walk east along the other side of the canal, we shall come on a track leading up to Scroop House?'

Without much suggesting pleasure at being thus appealed to, the young man nodded. He was about twenty-four, and Appleby saw at once that he was a young Binns. Thirty years on, he would be the image of his father. The girl, who was perhaps five years younger, was of a different type. And for a moment he wondered whether he had seen her somewhere before. But the slight air of familiarity she suggested was of the sort that is commonly illusory.

'Quite right,' the young man said – and gave Appleby a frank scowl. 'You come to a small wharf and a boat-house. The track goes up from there through the park. It used to be quite a road. You can't miss it.'

'We came down that way ourselves,' the girl said. This was plainly by way of continuing the conversation and making up for something approaching incivility in her brother. 'We are staying at Scroop House. As a matter of fact, we lived there once.'

'In fact, you are Daphne and Peter Binns.' Appleby shook hands, gave his name, and introduced the young people to Judith. 'If you are returning to the house,' he went on, 'perhaps we may walk up together. Colonel Raven has sent us to pay a call.' He smiled at the young Binnses – very much a courteous elderly man, accustomed to authority. 'As it happens, I feel not entirely a stranger to you. For I met your father last night.'

There was no mistaking the startled character of the swift glance the young Binnses exchanged on hearing this news.

'In London?' Peter Binns asked abruptly.

'At Pryde. Your father dropped in on Colonel Raven while motoring through. It was his first visit, I gathered, for some time. And he was in too much of a hurry to go on to Scroop.'

'Daddy never –' Daphne Binns had begun to say something which she thought better of. She checked herself – but only to plunge at something else. 'Wasn't it awful,' she said, 'about that old man – here, in the lock?'

'Tight, I expect. And fell and bashed his head.' Peter

Binns broke in with this roughly. 'But the police are making a stink about it. Earn their keep that way, I suppose.'

'And how do you earn your keep, Mr Binns?' Appleby asked this question in a tone sufficiently whimsical to make it inoffensive enough. But it put Peter Binns on his dignity.

'I have a position in my father's firm, sir,' he said.

'Gained,' Daphne Binns put in, 'by native merit and honest application. Signed, Daphne Binns.'

'You shut up,' Peter Binns said.

The Applebys, had they been the sort of people provided with eyebrows for such occasions, would no doubt have raised them. The manners of the young Binnses were unpolished. It was impossible to feel that the Grand Collector would have approved of them.

'Aren't you from the police?' Peter Binns suddenly demanded.

Appleby glanced at the young man in amusement. It was a fair enough question, although the manner of its being put was again not engaging. But Peter Binns was nervous as well as truculent. He was glancing sidelong at Appleby in a curiously uncertain way.

'Yes, I suppose I am – after a fashion, Mr Binns. But how did you know?'

'Oh, just the skivvies.'

'I beg your pardon?' It was so long since Appleby had heard this displeasing term used that he had actually failed to get hold of it.

'The servants, up at the house. Kitchen gossip. It's said that you're some sort of police inspector from London, and that just by chance you found this body. Have a nose for that sort of thing, I suppose.'

The Applebys could receive this only in silence. But Daphne Binns spoke up.

'The shocking thing is,' she said, 'that Peter doesn't mean

to be offensive. I mean, not more than usual. He's been to a public school, he's been to Cambridge, he held a commission during his National Service, and yet he's like this.'

'At least I'm not *pert*,' Peter said. 'And that's how I over-heard the vicar describing you to Dr West. A pert girl. So there. Signed, Peter Binns.'

After these exchanges, the party proceeded along the canal-bank in silence. Appleby was wondering how it came about that Bertram Coulson, if indeed a romantic idealist as Colonel Raven had declared, came to have these young people apparently as frequent guests. But he abandoned this speculation when he found himself on the small wharf which he had noticed earlier on the map.

'This is where Scroop House originally got its supplies,' he said to Judith. Then he turned to Peter Binns. 'Do you ever try the canal?' he asked. 'There seems to be a foot or so of water in this stretch. Do you keep any sort of craft in that boat-house?' And he nodded towards a small structure at the farther end of the wharf.

'Go on the canal?' Peter was surprised. 'The rotten old thing stinks, doesn't it? Even without having corpses dumped in it. As to whether there's anything in the boat-house, snoop for yourself. I never have.'

'I've peered in.' Daphne volunteered this in an almost conciliatory tone. 'There seems to be a big old punt, and I believe it's floating. But Mr Coulson or somebody keeps the place locked. Peter' – Daphne turned to challenge her brother – 'why do you keep on in that filthy way about the corpse? After all, you must remember the old man. I don't.'

'Your brother must certainly remember Crabtree.' Appleby interposed with this gravely. 'He would have been about nine when Crabtree went to America. Which means that you, Miss Binns, would have been three or four. Some people have quite a number of memories from that age. But you don't remember Seth Crabtree at all?'

'I certainly don't. I remember my nurse at that time. But this man was only somebody working out in the gardens or the stables, and naturally I wouldn't remember him. But Peter was always hanging around the servants' quarters. As a matter of fact, it's his thing now. Nothing really spectacular. He wouldn't have the nerve for that. Just pinching the bottoms of Mrs Coulson's maids, and thinking he's the hell of a dog.'

'Shut up,' Peter said. This time, he didn't say it particularly fiercely. It was almost as if he found mildly gratifying the light in which he had just been exhibited.

'And as a kid I gather he became quite a crony of this man Crabtree. Crabtree showed him all sorts of things.'

'Now, *will* you shut up, you ghastly little bitch?'

This time, the Applebys had difficulty in not stopping dead in their tracks. For Daphne had somehow contrived, with this last remark, to whip her brother into sudden fury. And into panic as well, Appleby thought, as he glanced at the young man. It was as if Daphne had made some treacherous move towards revealing a secret – and a secret so shabby, or so dirty, or even so criminal, that any approach to it scared Peter stiff. Yet that Peter had been no more than eight or nine at the time of Crabtree's departure was a fact which had just been agreed upon. What could Crabtree have shown such a child that should, in the retrospect, have such an effect on the grown man – if Peter Binns could be called a grown man – now? There were various unbeautiful possibilities, no doubt. And Appleby was far too case-hardened to have any difficulty in turning them over in his mind. But he was left with a feeling that his guesses were bad ones. Perhaps, with tact, a little genuine information could be got out of Peter himself.

'I see your sister somehow wants to make fun of you.' Appleby tried to speak with reassuring vagueness. 'But it's something that, as responsible men, we have to be serious about, don't you think? I know you lived here for many years, Mr Binns, and that you must have quite a position in the district. Many of the people round about here must still regard you as the young squire.'

'Quite right. Of course they do. Particularly as the Coulsons haven't an heir.' Peter Binns was much mollified.

'So when an affair like this turns up, people will naturally look to you to give a bit of a lead. In fact, you owe it to yourself to help the law in any way you can.'

'I suppose that's so.' Peter shot a far from trustful glance at Appleby. 'But it has nothing to do with me, all the same. I know nothing about Crabtree. Although naturally I do have a few memories of him from when I was a boy. Nothing much. But Daphne makes everything sound so damned silly.'

'We needn't bother about that.' Appleby continued to be soothing. 'I know that when your father became tenant here at Scroop, this man Crabtree stayed on. Would you say that it was in just the same capacity as in old Mrs Coulson's time?'

'How could I know anything about that?' Peter was definitely defensive again. 'I know nothing about that at all.'

'You see, I've picked up an impression – I don't quite know how – that Crabtree had some special position in old Mrs Coulson's scheme of things. Perhaps, even, he had some ascendancy over her.'

Judith interrupted here.

'I don't think that likely, at all. Mrs Coulson was clearly a person of very strong character, accustomed to boss rather a glittering scene. It isn't likely that a servant would gain an ascendancy over her.'

'It happened with Queen Victoria.' Daphne Binns offered

84

this – to the general surprise. 'And Crabtree may have had a lot of charm, or something.'

'I know nothing about him,' Peter reiterated obstinately. 'But I dare say he got in a lot of places where he shouldn't.'

Daphne Binns swung round on her brother.

'And just what do you mean by that, Peter?'

'I don't mean anything.'

'You don't mean anything. You don't know anything. And you don't signify anything, either. You're a mess. Signed –'

'But I think, Mr Binns, you did say you had a few memories of Crabtree.' Appleby had interrupted these unseemly children at their exchanges rather brusquely. 'Are you sure they are entirely irrelevant to the puzzle of his death?'

'Of course they are. I remember that he made me a sledge. I suppose my father told him to.'

'Perhaps he did. Or perhaps Crabtree just happened to like making a sledge for a boy. Did he take you poaching?'

'Why should he take me poaching? My father had the sporting rights of the whole place.'

'Well, there was Colonel Raven's estate next door. A boy might find it fun to be taken over there on a dark night.'

'I don't expect that, as a boy, Peter was much of an outdoor type.' Daphne had interrupted. 'He had a splendid collection of birds' eggs. He still has them, because he hates letting anything go. But – do you know? – he bought them all out of a catalogue from some shop in London. He had a whole museum which impressed me very much – until I found out he'd bought everything in it. I can't think where he got the money from.'

'Can't you keep quiet?' Peter demanded. 'Yes, when I come to think of it, Crabtree did show me how to snare rabbits, and things like that.'

Appleby had come to a halt – apparently to admire the

south front of Scroop House, which was now in full view. He seemed even to have become more interested in this than in the conversation, so casually did his next question drop from him.

'So did you look forward to seeing him again?'

'Not in the –' Peter Binns checked himself. 'What do you mean?' he demanded. 'I knew nothing about him.'

'But I understand that Mr Coulson ran into him yesterday morning, and that Crabtree gave an account of himself. Mr Coulson proposed to see him again, and perhaps find him work. Didn't this crop up – perhaps in talk before lunch, or round about then?'

There was a moment's silence. Peter and Daphne Binns – who, if conspirators, were unaccomplished ones – glanced at each other swiftly and blankly.

'Oh, yes,' Peter said. His manner was at once careless and awkward. 'Mr Coulson mentioned it when he came in from his morning prowl. We all heard it: Mrs Coulson, Hollywood, everybody.'

'Hollywood knew already,' Appleby said. 'Because Crabtree had called at the house earlier in the morning.'

'You seem to know a damned lot about us.' Peter Binns scowled at Appleby.

'Do you think so?' Appleby shook his head, and began moving again towards Scroop House. 'To be quite frank with you, I feel I've a lot still to learn.'

'But I don't see,' Daphne Binns said, 'that you're going to learn much by coming to Scroop. I mean, about this dead man. Peter has these vague memories, I have none at all, and neither of the Coulsons can ever have set eyes on Crabtree. They didn't live here for ages, you know. First there was old Mrs Coulson, who employed the man. Then there was Daddy as Mr Coulson's tenant, and he employed the man too. But a few years after that, it seems that the man went to

America or somewhere. It was only after that again that we left, and the Coulsons moved in. So there's no reason to suppose that the Coulsons had as much as heard of the man until he turned up yesterday. It doesn't look as if you'll get much out of *them*.'

'Possibly not.' Appleby had listened patiently to Daphne's rather plodding speech. 'But, you see, one never can be *sure* that one won't get something out of people. And it's possible I may get something more out of you.'

'What do you mean?'

'Even if it's only an opinion or a guess.' Daphne, Appleby thought, had the same liability as her brother towards sudden alarm and even panic. 'What do you think would make an old man like this turn up again as Crabtree did yesterday?'

'He'd come for what he could get.' Daphne's alarm had melted oddly into a sort of savage vehemence. 'Or do you think that he just had nice feelings about a golden past, and was anxious to see how the roses were continuing to grow round the door – or if Peter had grown up into a fine up-standing English gentleman? I think not. He was a crook who thought he had a line on somebody.'

'What awful rubbish!' Peter broke in with a savagery of his own, and with a glare at his sister as if she had committed some utterly crass blunder. 'He was just some old peasant with a superstitious notion that he should die and be buried in his own village. And some tramp came along and obliged him – probably for the sake of robbing the corpse of a pocket-ful of small change. Why all this fuss over a common-or-garden squalid crime, with top coppers getting foot-loose from Scotland Yard, I just can't think.'

Appleby stopped in his tracks once more. But this time, he surveyed not the house but the young man who was con-ducting him to it.

'Mr Binns,' he said, 'I must confess that your manners

87

are not agreeable to me. At the same time, you are talking tolerable sense. Undesigned homicide in the course of a too carelessly perpetrated robbery with violence is, statistically, far the most probable explanation of Crabtree's death. Your sister's notion, on the other hand, is an odd and quirky one.'

'There!' Peter said, turning to Daphne. 'Sucks to you!'

Appleby ignored this puerility.

'But I ought to add that it is what your sister says that interests me, all the same.'

After this the party had walked for some minutes in silence. Scroop House was now directly in front of them. On their right it was almost impinged on by a beech copse. On their left there appeared to be a walled garden. But straight in front the park ran directly up to a low balustraded terrace before the house. The façade, as the Applebys had previously seen from a distance, was plain to the point of bleakness. But the proportions were good, and the total effect was impressive as well as pleasing. Old Mrs Coulson, who had, it seemed, gone in so uncompromisingly only for the best people and the best things, had possessed an admirable backdrop to her activities in Scroop House. Mr Arthur Balfour himself, in point of severe good taste, must often have compared the place favourably with a good many of the grand houses among which, with his fellow Cabinet Ministers, he was accustomed to revolve at week-ends.

Judith was delighted. It was clear that Seth Crabtree – although she had been so disposed to make a pet of him – was banished for a time from her head, now that this not readily accessible masterpiece by William Chambers was actually before her.

A figure had appeared on the terrace: the figure of a woman holding a small watering-can, with which she was tending a line of plants disposed along the balustrade. Here, plainly, was the lady of the house. And Appleby, although not much given to a sentimental regard for places of this kind, acknowledged something pleasing and obscurely moving in this modest domestic spectacle. Just so had the womenfolk of Scroop House been pottering around since Chambers rolled up his drawings, dismissed his workmen, and handed the place over to the first Coulson in 1786.

They had all come to a halt again – and Appleby realized that, this time, it was Daphne Binns who had brought this about.

'It's Mrs Coulson,' Daphne said. Her voice had altered. 'She's nice. In fact, you'll find her no end of a pleasant change. Peter, march!' And Daphne gave her brother a sharp nudge in the ribs. Then she looked straight at the Applebys. 'Exeunt the bloody Binnses,' she said. 'Signed, Daphne Binns.'

Chapter Eight

'Would you call them *enfants terribles*?' Judith asked, as they watched the young Binnses make off towards a corner of the house.

'I don't know.' Appleby shook his head. 'But I do know I'm sorry I said something pompous to the boy about his manners. I'm not a damned adjutant or house master or moral tutor.'

'You're a Commissioner of Police, John, and getting dangerously accustomed to deference. But you were quite right, all the same. He was unspeakable. And his sister wasn't much better.'

'I don't know that I agree. The boy is certainly one of nature's Binnses, and Harrer an' Trinity College haven't much changed him.'

'Whatever are you talking about?'

'A poem of Kipling's. Don't forget your plain policeman's simple tastes. But what I'm saying is that the girl is a cut above the boy. I liked her.'

'Yes, she's not bad looking, I agree.'

'Idiot. Or – as Peter would say – shut up. There's more to Daphne than to her brother. And she's more dangerous.'

'The female of the species is more deadly than the male. Your friend Kipling again. But go on.'

'Peter is up against something rather small, and Daphne is up against something pretty big. Of course, small things, just as much as big ones, lead to rash acts from time to time. I wonder when their mother died.'

'You know she's dead?'

'Well, she vanished and didn't turn up again. And it's

only the dead who don't, sooner or later, turn up. Anyway, Mrs Binns's virtual non-existence seems to be the explanation of the children's coming here from time to time. They've found a mother – don't you think? – in the lady of the watering-can. Your uncle says she has a roving eye. But I suspect she had a maternal instinct as well. And she's coming down those steps to meet us now.'

There was no doubt that Colonel Raven's description of Bertram Coulson's wife, although it had been couched in somewhat Edwardian terms, fitted the lady very well. She was a devilish fine woman in a mature way. But if there was indeed a smothered fire in her, or at least a suggestion that she had difficulty in finding the life laid down for her adequate to her sense of what life should provide, this was less immediately striking than an entirely pleasing quickness of response and warmth of interest. She had still been carrying her watering-can when she came down to greet her visitors. Now, back on the terrace, she walked them about for a few minutes, talking about her plants, before settling them in a sunny corner. This last action she performed competently, but with a certain vagueness as to the disposition of chairs and cushions which struck Appleby as a revealing characteristic at once. He doubted whether Mrs Coulson was much of a housewife, or managed any very effective contact with the inanimate world around her. She was a kind of *magna mater* whose true sphere was a teeming nursery with all its proper appendages of ponies, puppies, kittens and canaries. Lacking these, she might conceivably get wrong what it was she did lack. And a mistake of that sort might take her into difficult waters.

'My husband has had to go over to the farm,' she said, 'but he will be back quite soon. It is something to do with the milking parlour.'

'Why does one have milking parlours?' Judith, whom Appleby judged liable to start conversations on too brittle a metropolitan note, looked interrogatively at Mrs Coulson. 'Stable boys make those odd noises when grooming horses, but do milkmaids converse with cows?'

'I'm afraid I have never thought about it. We must ask Bertram. He is very proud of knowing everything about English country ways.' Mrs Coulson paused, as if seeking some way of carrying on the topic. 'In my own country we have a saying – or it may be a song, for I don't quite remember – about singing to the cattle. But that is not, perhaps, quite the same thing. The point about the milking parlour, I think, is that it has to meet certain standards before Bertram is allowed to market the milk in a certain way. Bertram has letters about it from the Ministry of Agriculture and Fisheries. Not that we market fish.' Mrs Coulson paused again. 'Does Colonel Raven market fish?'

Judith laughed. Having received a frown from her husband, she was obediently dropping her conversational pitch.

'I don't think so – although fish are almost the only thing he talks about. Do Mr Coulson and he have angling as a topic in common?'

'Oh, certainly they do. Bertram has all the topics he feels he ought to have. He does everything. Did you know, Lady Appleby, that there is something called the Country Gentlemen's Association?'

'I don't think I did. But there ought to be, so I suppose there is.' Judith was conscious of receiving another frown from Appleby as a reward for this idiocy. 'And Mr Coulson belongs?'

'I believe he is on some sort of council or committee. My husband, you see, was a little diffident about coming to live at Scroop. Having nerved himself to it, he does nothing half-heartedly.'

'That's very sensible,' Appleby said. He was coming to feel that Mrs Coulson, as one might say, decidedly knew what was in her flower-pots. And a critical spirit lurked in her. For that matter, something less readily distinguishable lurked in her as well. In fact, it suddenly came to Appleby that he was enjoying the Crabtree affair very much. There was no dead wood in it. There were no supers – no mere walking-on parts. Everybody was at least worth observation. 'So I take it,' he went on, 'that Mr Coulson is very much a practical farmer?'

'Yes, indeed. He is very much against what he calls sur-tax farming. And week-end squires.'

'I suppose his former tenant, Mr Binns, was something of a week-end squire?'

'My husband did eventually rather fall out with Mr Binns.' Suddenly, Mrs Coulson was speaking with caution. 'But I don't think that, to this day, he really knows why he did so. Something bad, you see, happened in the Binnses' home.'

'Yes, I've heard of that.'

'And Bertram hated it. Bertram hated that happening in a home where – where there were children.' Mrs Coulson had again changed her manner, as if resolved upon frankness. 'You see?'

'Yes, I see.'

'And he would have liked Scroop to have a direct heir. That – although he scarcely knows it – is why he agrees to having the young Binnses here from time to time.'

'We walked up from the canal with them,' Judith said. 'We found them – most interesting.'

'Yes, of course.' Mrs Coulson gave Judith a glance which wasn't exactly uncomprehending. 'And I like having them simply because they lost their mother when so young. I have thought I might be more to them than I have turned out to be.'

'Don't be too sure.' What Appleby thought of as her social manner had suddenly dropped from Judith. She spoke gently and seriously. 'You are rather important to Daphne Binns.'

'You think so?' Mrs Coulson had flushed faintly. 'There are things one learns too late.'

Silence followed this – as it will when casual acquaintances have gone a step too deep. Mrs Coulson looked out over the terrace, as if hoping that her husband might now turn up. But the park was empty. And its emptiness seemed to drive Mrs Coulson to further confidence.

'And there is the fact,' she said, 'that this house is haunted.' She smiled at what must have been Judith's look of alarm. 'Perhaps you are thinking of poor Mrs Binns, who disappeared so oddly. But it's nothing like that. I don't speak literally, Lady Appleby. Scroop is haunted only for my husband. And by the last Mrs Coulson.'

'The Grand Collector?'

'They called her that.' There was a trace of impatience in the present Mrs Coulson's voice. 'I suppose she was a re-markable woman. Scroop House appears in the books of that period – in the biographies and memoirs of famous people.'

Appleby, who had been listening in silence, himself for some reason felt impatient at this point.

'Perhaps it does,' he said, ' – here and there. But I suspect that local legend exaggerates that aspect of the place, if I may say so. And I hope your husband doesn't put in a lot of time sighing over past glories that are mainly in his own head.'

Whether this forthright and not entirely civil speech was calculated or not, it had a decided effect upon Mrs Coulson.

'But he does!' she said. 'And yet he is quite as able a man as Alfred Binns. He would have gone farther, by a long way.

I mean, at the sort of thing men like to do. Nobody knew more about packing meat. He was all set to put Australia right away ahead. But he had to have this. And it hasn't worked – or not really. I don't know why. But I sometimes think he doesn't, for some reason, feel entitled to be at Scroop at all.'

'How very odd!' Judith said – rather at random, and by way of breaking another silence.

'I sometimes think it *makes* people odd. Certainly it did no good to Alfred Binns. And old Mrs Coulson is said to have turned very queer in the end. Of course she had reached a great age. She turned secretive, I understand. But here comes Bertram.'

Appleby eyed with considerable curiosity the figure now hurrying down the terrace towards them. But, although the figure was indeed making very good speed, 'hurrying' was not the precisely appropriate word. 'Loping' might be better. Bertram Coulson was tall and lean, with a slight stoop. His possession of these features was enhanced by his being dressed in a Norfolk jacket which only just stopped short of a length suggesting a hunting-coat, knickerbockers which hovered between being breeches and the species of garment vulgarly known in Appleby's youth as 'plus-fours', and leggings with the dull polish that comes from the careful scouring and burnishing away of many impositions of mud and loam. And Bertram Coulson carried a shooting-stick. It was not, perhaps, an object with which many gentlemen equip themselves for the purpose of strolling to and from a home farm. But it did contribute to the general effect. So did the lope. It seemed to suggest somebody who is never more at home than when striding across ploughland on some urgent bucolic occasion.

Not – Appleby at once added to himself in justice – that there was anything that could be called absurd about

95

Bertram Coulson. He was a good-looking man, and the clothes that did somehow catch the eye were good-looking clothes too; his tweed had plainly reached him from the Hebrides by way of Savile Row. There wasn't about him – as there had been about Mr David Channing-Kennedy of the Jolly Leggers – any suggestion of the spurious. He was simply a man who had taken on a role, and who remained a little conscious of the fact.

'Lady Appleby? How do you do.' Bertram Coulson advanced to shake hands, became aware that the result of this gesture was to offer Judith the shooting-stick, rectified the error hastily, and then turned to Appleby. 'Sir John, how do you do. I must apologize to Lady Appleby for not being on the spot. Good of Raven to persuade you to come over. He's a very good neighbour of mine. We hit it off pretty well on one local matter and another. Both believe in keeping an eye on things. Many of them are a neglectful lot about here, I'm sorry to say. Up and down to London by train, spend the week-ends with their noses in financial journals, and scarcely know their own people by sight. Sad state of affairs. But how is your uncle, Lady Appleby? I gathered he'd had another touch of gout. Stood thigh-deep in too many rivers in his time, I suppose. But worth it, after all. No peace like the peace you get flogging a decent stretch of water.'

Various civilities succeeded upon this speech. Mrs Coulson's contributions to these were adequate but not prominent. In her husband's presence she seemed inclined to withdraw into the position of a spectator. And Appleby thought that her attitude to Coulson was tinged with an ironical quality that one would scarcely have predicted from the general warmth and simplicity of her personality.

'The reason I'm late,' Coulson went on, 'is simply that, as Edith may have told you, I'm a bit of a practical farmer nowadays. I went over to see about flooring the milking parlour of my own little concern. And it occurred to me' – Coulson turned to his wife – 'that it might be a good time to concrete the farther yard. There are times of the year when Bridges has to bring in his cows from the twelve-acre through a couple of feet of mud. And mud' – this time Coulson turned to Judith – 'is bad for muck, wouldn't you say?'

'Oh, yes – indeed.' Judith was all grave assent. 'Concrete a yard, and you begin to get some of the cost back in muck in no time. I'm so glad you're sound on manure.'

Coulson was delighted. But Mrs Coulson – Appleby noted – was regarding Judith with a sceptical eye.

'I don't remember,' Mrs Coulson said, 'that Bertram was so enthusiastic about the manure, or would have entertained visitors with it so speedily, when he was an overlander.'

'An overlander?' Appleby said.

'*The* overlander, in the end.' Mrs Coulson spoke with a touch of affectionate pride. 'Whenever they ate a steak in Melbourne or Adelaide – and they begin, you know, eating them at breakfast and go on all day – Bertram had brought it to them on the hoof. And he was in at the death, too.'

Coulson laughed.

'By the death,' he said, 'Edith means the big freeze. We stopped herding them down that murderous thousand miles, and started slaughtering and freezing them on the spot. Technical advances made it the logical thing. But it took – well, it took all the romance away.'

Judith nodded sagely – so that Appleby had a gloomy vision of her making a pet of this Bertram Coulson rather in the way she had been disposed to do with the late Seth Crabtree. He hoped that another prompt fatality wouldn't ensue.

'But there's still some romance,' Judith asked, 'in concreting that yard, and thinking about the twelve-acre, and

– well, in living where Coulsons have lived for a long time?'

Appleby wondered whether Mrs Coulson's toes were curling as his were at this outrageous appeal to sentiment. Not that Judith wasn't doing her bit. They weren't, after all, honest payers of a morning call. They were snoopers, as young Mr Peter Binns had roundly suggested. And Judith was simply prodding Bertram Coulson to see how he would respond.

He didn't, in fact, respond with any very direct reply: rather, he gave the impression of something like a nervous shying away from the theme of Coulson succeeding Coulson.

'I certainly arranged about the yard to my satisfaction, Lady Appleby. But then I was held up by something else. A fellow called Hilliard, our local police inspector, rang me up.' Coulson turned to Appleby and gave him a straight glance – the kind of straight glance, Appleby thought, that is planned that way a second before it happens. 'It was about this poor fellow Crabtree.'

'The man who had the fatal accident yesterday?' It was Mrs Coulson who asked this.

'Yes, my dear – at the lock. Hilliard is coming up to make some inquiries. As you know, I ran into the old man yesterday. It must have been only a few hours before he died.'

'And it was my wife and I who found the body,' Appleby said. It wasn't clear to him whether Bertram Coulson already knew this. 'Has Hilliard in fact told you that Crabtree's death was accidental?'

'Well, no. His mind seems to be running on foul play. But policemen are obliged to think of such things.' Coulson checked himself, and made what appeared to be a spontaneous gesture of apology. 'But I really forgot, Sir John, that you must yourself, I suppose, be called a policeman.'

Appleby felt that it was his turn to offer a straight glance, and at the same time make it explicit that in fact he wasn't paying a merely social call.

'Of course,' he said, 'I have no standing in this affair at all. Or not officially. But, as it happens, I have spent the better part of my career in criminal investigation. So when I happen to stumble upon what may be a crime, the local police take it for granted that I'll give them a hand if I can. Something of the sort is plainly in this man Hilliard's head. And I have to confess that an unsolved mystery acts as a kind of irritant on me. I want to scratch. So wherever I go at the moment – Scroop House or anywhere else – I shall be thinking about Crabtree's death, and looking round for any light I can get on it. This is rather an awkward thing to say. But it must be said.'

There was a short silence. Mrs Coulson employed it in remarking a drooping plant on the balustrade, rising, watering it, and returning composedly to her chair.

'Quite right,' Bertram Coulson said. 'If there's a mystery about this man's death, I'm glad you're here to look into it. We don't want anything of a dubious nature going unquestioned, I assure you. Bad for local feeling. Of course I'm a magistrate and so forth, as well as passing pretty tolerably as the squire, and perhaps I can say without impertinence that your help is welcome.'

'Thank you.' Appleby felt that Coulson had come rather well out of this. 'And I'm afraid we can't very lightly dismiss the possibility of foul play. Frankly, I don't see how Crabtree's injuries could have been accidentally occasioned.'

'Well, I've been down to the lock, and I think I do. It's astonishing, the queer things that can happen through sheer misadventure and accident. I've seen a good many in Australia. And I don't doubt that you've seen a good many nearer home.'

'That's perfectly true.'

'Take something I was reading of the other day. An American on a golf course. Millionaire, as it happens, which is why it hit the headlines. Took a swipe with one of those steel clubs, broke it, and contrived to have it pierce his groin, so that he died on the spot. Unbelievable, wouldn't you say?'

'Oh, how horrible!' Mrs Coulson had sprung to her feet, knocking over her watering-can with a clatter. She instantly sat down again. 'Forgive me! Bertram, is there any point in your telling us of such a thing?'

'My dear Edith, I am so sorry!' Coulson appeared genuinely concerned. 'I wanted merely to remind Sir John that one sometimes hears of very unlikely accidents indeed. And at least I shall continue to hope that Crabtree wasn't murdered. His death is sufficiently upsetting even if due to natural causes. He had come back to Scroop – and out of the most admirable local piety, I believe. Yesterday I met him, and I liked him. He was elderly, but I should certainly have found him employment. I blame myself that I didn't inquire more particularly about his immediate circumstances, and perhaps offer him a bed in the servants' wing.'

'I rather gather,' Appleby said, 'that you had never met him before, since he went off to America while the Binnses were still here at Scroop. But had you heard of him?'

'It depends what you mean.' Coulson appeared to be gaining confidence with Appleby. 'I don't believe, as it happens, that I ever heard anybody speak of him. Peter Binns may have done so, but I don't remember anything of the sort. But, all the same, Crabtree wasn't a complete surprise to me. I'd read about him.'

For a moment this statement seemed entirely odd. Seth Crabtree had not, perhaps, been a wholly commonplace person. But Judith at least, who had placed him so securely in the context of Gray's *Elegy*, was disposed to see him as eminently a youth to fortune and to fame unknown. Nor did Appleby see how he could well have been written about.

'You must take a glance at my books.' Suddenly Coulson was speaking with diffidence. 'I have pretty well everything, I think, in which this old place is mentioned. Not, of course, that it *is* old.'

'1786,' Judith said.

'Quite right.' Coulson was pleased. 'There was, as a matter of fact, a Jacobean house, built by an earlier Coulson. For what it's worth, I may mention that he had been Speaker of the House of Commons.' There was a faint quiver in Coulson's voice as he casually announced this. 'But the family went rather to pot in the later seventeenth century, and the house became ruinous and simply disappeared. It was pretty well as a new man that a fellow called Bertram Coulson, who had restored the family fortunes as a merchant in Bristol, called in William Chambers to build *this* house.' Coulson turned in his chair, so that he had a view of his inheritance. 'In its plain way, it's not too bad, wouldn't you say?'

'I love it, Mr Coulson.' Judith said this honestly enough. 'But you were saying that you have most of the books that have any mention of Scroop.'

'Ah, yes – I was forgetting. And this poor fellow Crabtree comes in. Quite casually, that is to say, in the memoirs of two or three people who record visits to the place in old Sara Coulson's time.'

'You mean that Crabtree was a sort of character among the servants, and got mentioned as being quaint or humorous or something of that sort?'

'Almost that. But not quite.' Coulson seemed anxious to be precise. 'He had some sort of position with the old lady. People felt that she relied on him. It was something like that. Nobody makes much of it. But it had caught my eye as I read. And I remembered about it as soon as Crabtree mentioned his name to me yesterday.'

'Do any of the books,' Appleby asked, 'say anything about your butler?'

'Hollywood?' Coulson was surprised. 'Why should they? Ah, but I forgot. He is, of course, our link with the old lady. He was with her for some years, and stayed on with Binns and later with ourselves. But Hollywood is an unnoticeable man. Nobody would think to mention Hollywood in a book. Don't you agree, Edith?'

'Yes, I do agree.' Mrs Coulson was glancing along the terrace. 'But I think it will have occurred to Sir John that Hollywood may be able to tell him something about this unfortunate dead man in the old days. If, that is to say, his death really calls for inquiry into the past history of Scroop. And here is Hollywood coming now.'

An elderly man was advancing down the terrace, carrying a silver tray. And Bertram Coulson noted this with approval. He turned to Judith.

'Ah, yes,' he said. 'A glass of Madeira, Lady Appleby. It's our habit at this hour.'

Chapter Nine

Appleby's first glance at the Coulsons' butler was taken, not unnaturally, in the light of his colleague Tarbox's lurid portrait of his past. For here, if Tarbox was to be believed, was a retired – presumably a retired – Tarquin: the ravisher, or at least seducer, of bevies of female domestics now known at Scroop no more.

One would scarcely, Appleby decided, have guessed anything of the sort. Indeed, confronted with Hollywood, one would have felt very little sanguine of guessing anything at all. He was a spare man of indefinite age, parchment-like pallor, and absolute immobility of countenance. Unlike Tarbox, who, beneath a convention of impassivity was both communicative and cordially disposed, Hollywood was the sort of servant who admits no shadow of personal relationship with his employers. Appleby, judging him unattractive, thought it odd that he should have survived through three successive régimes at Scroop. Old Mrs Coulson must first have engaged or promoted him, and perhaps her notions of the grand manner had included servants like automata. Alfred Binns, whose social origins were presumably simple, might have kept him on as a man who at least usefully knew all the local ropes. But it was more surprising that Bertram Coulson, who was simple only in a more subtle and idiosyncratic way, should have kept him on as well. For one would somehow expect the present proprietor of Scroop to have in his mind, as appropriate to this particular employment, a man capable of a little more personal warmth, and better answering to the traditional notion of a family retainer, than the grim and grey person now disposing a decanter and glasses on a table beside his employer.

'Just a moment, Hollywood.' Bertram Coulson spoke briskly and pleasantly. His feeling of inadequacy as the inheritor of Scroop, if it really existed, certainly didn't extend to awkwardness with servants. 'A Mr Hilliard, an inspector of police, is coming up later this morning in connexion with the man who was found dead yesterday. It seems likely that there will be extensive inquiries. And my guest here, Sir John Appleby, who is a great authority on such matters, is also interested.'

'Yes, sir?' Hollywood, after offering his employer this response in a chilly tone, turned and offered Appleby an equally chilly bow.

'Well, Hollywood' – for a moment Coulson seemed to feel for an opening – 'I think you must remember something of this man Crabtree in the old days?'

'I remember him, sir.'

'And you recognized him when he came up to the house yesterday?'

'Yes and no, sir. I had a feeling that he was somebody who had worked about the place long ago. And a little more came back to me later.'

'May I mention something?' Appleby interposed. 'Crabtree seemed to feel that you were unresponsive.'

'It may have been so, sir. I had a feeling that he was not a man up to much good.'

'That is most interesting.' Appleby, who was now being handed a glass of Madeira, looked steadily at Hollywood. 'Did you feel that he had come here for the purpose of making some troublesome application to Mr Coulson?'

'Yes, sir. That was my feeling. It was not a matter of anything the man said, but rather of his manner. There was something he was proposing to presume on. I felt that there was even a suggestion of a threat.'

'A threat, Hollywood?' It was Mrs Coulson who spoke. And there was something new in her voice. 'This was yesterday morning?'

'Yes, madam. Shortly before eleven o'clock.'

There was a short silence. Appleby took a sip at his Madeira – of which he didn't, at this hour, propose to drink much.

'I'm trying,' he said, 'to get a clear picture of Crabtree's standing in the late Mrs Coulson's household. Can you help me there?'

'He had none, sir. He was an outdoor man.'

'No doubt. But there is evidence that Mrs Coulson held him in some regard. This must be something you know about, I think – if you will just try to remember.'

Hollywood produced his most aloof bow.

'I believe I do, sir. Mrs Coulson judged Crabtree to have taste. In the gardens in general. But particularly with herbaceous borders. He became rather a tyrant, I believe, in matters of that sort.'

Bertram Coulson shook his head impatiently.

'This doesn't seem to be getting us very far,' he said. 'And my own impression of Crabtree yesterday doesn't support Hollywood's in the least. I found nothing troublesome in him, and certainly no suggestion of a threat.'

'I am very glad to hear it, sir.' Hollywood's tone was excessively smooth. 'I must have been mistaken, of course. Can I be of any further assistance?'

'Everybody must try to be that, Hollywood.' For the first time, Bertram Coulson spoke a shade sharply. 'Sir John knows that I am not convinced that anything criminal or sinister has occurred. But, if the police think otherwise, they are likely to be right. It's their business to be so. And now, Hollywood, here is the plain fact. As long as the affair is a mystery, none of us is beyond suspicion. Or that's my reading of the matter. Appleby, am I right?'

Appleby nodded. Whatever the origin – he was thinking – of the curious uncertainty that lurked deep in Coulson, the man had a thoroughly sound intelligence. His wife was probably not wrong in the supposition that, had not Scroop House turned up on him, he would have gone even farther than he had in the matter of packing meat.

'Yes,' Appleby said. 'That's fair enough. Hilliard will want to question everybody – and he's entitled to. I want to do the same thing – and I'm not.'

Mrs Coulson, who had been silent for some time, and whose gaze had been rather wistfully on her watering-can, was moved to speech by this.

'What kind of questions, Sir John?'

'Some rather crude ones, I'm afraid. But please realize that they may very well turn out to be entirely irrelevant. Crabtree, as has been suggested to me, may have been killed by some ruffian totally unknown to any of us, and as a mere matter of petty robbery. But, until some positive evidence to that effect appears, we have to explore other assumptions. He worked here long ago. He comes back and contacts the place. Within a matter of hours, he is killed. We must consider the implications of that.'

'You mean' – Mrs Coulson hesitated – 'that the explanation of his death lies far back in the history of Scroop?'

'I consider that possibility – among others.'

'I see.' Very curiously, Mrs Coulson uttered an uncontrolled gasp or sigh. It might have been of apprehension, or it might have been of relief. It might even have betokened a confused mingling of these emotions. Or – Appleby told himself out of long experience – it might have no significance at all, except as a reminder that the most innocent of English gentlewomen may be subject to a modicum of emotional distress when suddenly brought hard up against a violent crime.

'The first and elementary questions,' Appleby went on, 'concern the time at which Crabtree died, and the account that each individual can give of how he was employing himself – and in whose company, if any – at the relevant period.'

At this, Coulson gave a harsh laugh.

'Well,' he said, 'I call that crude enough. But it's plain good sense, as well. We'd better begin – and have our information ready for Hilliard. Ought we to have the young people along?'

'Peter and Daphne?' Mrs Coulson, who had abandoned the study of her watering-can in favour of an absent glance into empty space, turned alert at this. 'I don't think we want any effect of summoning them, Bertram. We have, of course, known them from childhood. But they remain our guests. If Mr Hilliard wishes to question them when he arrives, let him do so.'

'I am sure you are quite right, Edith.' Coulson turned to Appleby. 'May we know, for a start, just when Crabtree is supposed to have died? Or is that to go about the matter the wrong way round?'

'Not at all. Let us begin there, by all means. And it is very much Judith's and my own part in the affair. We were talking to Crabtree at one o'clock. He left us at approximately one-twenty. We saw his body in the lock at precisely one-fifty-eight. Take the distance from the Jolly Leggers to the lock into account, and you will see that we have a tight time-schedule on our hands. Nobody can have been directly concerned in his death who can account for his, or her, movements during a crucial twenty minutes which these times indicate. And it's a twenty minutes, I should imagine, during which this household would have been in each other's presence at luncheon.'

'One-forty onwards?' Bertram Coulson asked this question slowly and with a new severity of accent.

'Precisely that,' Appleby said.

'Then luncheon doesn't help. We have it at twelve-thirty at this time of year. And yesterday, for some reason, it was a somewhat perfunctory and hasty affair. I know I was out in the park by one o'clock. I had one or two things to think over – and did the job on a solitary walk. The rest of us were probably dispersed by the same hour. Wouldn't that be right, Hollywood?'

'You forget, sir, that I did not serve luncheon yesterday. I instructed Evans to do so. I was engaged in checking over the table-linen, since the mistress and I were to consider replacements.'

'By yourself?' Appleby asked.

'Certainly, sir. But I was joined by the mistress at half past one, and we were then in the linen room together until a little after two o'clock.' Hollywood turned to Mrs Coulson. 'That, madam, I think would be correct?'

For a moment Mrs Coulson, who had returned to studying space, made no reply.

'You would confirm the hour, madam?' There was no trace of urgency or anxiety in Hollywood's voice.

'Yes, Hollywood – of course.'

Mrs Coulson, too, spoke without excitement. But she was looking at her husband's butler, Appleby thought, as if she had never seen him before.

'That takes us some way, then,' Bertram Coulson said. And he in his turn spoke calmly. It came to Appleby that Mrs Coulson's having established an *alibi* – or her having an *alibi* established for her – meant absolutely nothing to her husband. And this was not because of indifference. It was because it would never have occurred to him to suspect her for a moment of complicity in anything resembling crime. 'And now,' Coulson went on, 'it really is only the children whom Sir John may want to talk to. Unless, that is, all the servants are to be considered as in the picture.'

'They'll be in Hilliard's picture,' Appleby said. 'I don't think they need be in mine.' He paused. There had been something in the way Coulson had said 'the children' making it clear that Alfred Binns's not wholly engaging son and daughter enjoyed almost an adoptive position here at Scroop. 'Peter and Daphne,' he asked, 'come here a good deal?'

'Yes – and we are always glad to have them. They are, you know, motherless. Edith' – Coulson glanced at his wife – 'has always tried to do what she could, particularly for the girl. But it was the boy who, at first, used to be keener on coming back here.'

'He enjoys country life and sports?' Judith asked.

'I don't know that one could say that.' Bertram Coulson sounded faintly puzzled. 'He likes a little shooting. In fact there he is, going after the pigeons again now.'

The figure of Peter Binns had appeared at a corner of the house. He was carrying a gun and making for the wood.

'Do you know,' Appleby said casually, 'that I think I'll go and try to mend my acquaintance with him? Would that be all right?'

'By all means.' Bertram Coulson rose. 'And perhaps Lady Appleby would care to see the house?' He turned to Judith. 'Edith and I will be delighted to show it to you.'

Appleby saw Judith react most favourably to this suggestion. It was in unexpected circumstances, he reflected, that she was fulfilling her ambition of inspecting the interior of Scroop. He had a notion that he ought perhaps to inspect it too. But that would keep. So he made some polite remark to Mrs Coulson and descended from the terrace on the trail of young Binns.

But for some minutes it was Mrs Coulson who stuck in his head. Outwardly she was composed enough: a woman poised over and in control of a familiar environment – an environment acknowledged in her heart, perhaps, to be irksome or inadequate, but an environment accepted and made the best of, nevertheless. That was certainly the normal Edith Coulson, for many years the mistress of Scroop House. But, beneath this, was there another woman – one who had lately, and to her own bewilderment, visited a different world? Appleby didn't know. He could only take note that something indefinable about Bertram Coulson's wife had raised this speculation in his mind.

'It's you, is it?' Peter Binns had delivered himself of this on swinging round and discovering Appleby behind him.

'Yes – and I must really apologize. But it is the hunter's instinct, Mr Binns' – and Appleby glanced at the weapon in Peter Binns's hands – 'so perhaps you will forgive me. It's true I'm not after pigeons. I'm after a killer.'

'I don't believe this old man was murdered.'

'I'm afraid I do. And I want to find the murderer. I begin by ruling people out. I know when Crabtree died. So I check up on people's movements and whereabouts at that time. You see?'

Not perhaps without justification, Peter Binns took offence at this question.

'Look,' he said, 'I'm not utterly a moron – although you seem to have me typed as that. I suppose it's because of the way you heard Daphne talking to me.'

'I don't know that I concluded much from that. Are you fond of your sister?'

Again with justification, Peter Binns was outraged.

'What the hell do you mean?' he demanded. And then, curiously, he added: 'I wouldn't want the young idiot to have too rough a spin.'

'No, of course not.' Appleby took this smoothly. 'By the way, I suppose you were out after the pigeons during this half hour or so that I'm interested in?'

'If you mean just after lunch yesterday, sir, you're quite right. I was.'

'And lunch ended rather early?'

'Yes. It was a dismal sort of meal. Everybody feeling glum.'

'Because of Crabtree?'

Peter Binns's face took on its panic-stricken look.

'What do you mean – because of Crabtree?'

'I think you'd all heard that this old man had just turned up out of the past, so to speak. Would that be why you were all glum?'

'Do you mean that we all had secrets which this old man might tell about?'

'That is a possibility. Or perhaps just one secret which was of some concern to all of you. What did your sister do after this glum lunch?'

'She said she was going to her room to write a letter.'

'Was that quite usual?'

'I don't think Daphne often writes letters. You're too interested in Daphne, by a long way. She's nineteen. You don't think that a girl like that suddenly walked out and killed somebody, do you?'

'Put like that, Mr Binns, it sounds most improbable. It's even mildly improbable that *you* did, you know. I shouldn't say that large and uncontrollable passions are your line. But perhaps you have a stock of little ones.'

'Didn't you say that you didn't like my manners? I don't like yours.' Peter Binns had flushed. 'And they're not even natural to you – as mine, for what they're worth, are to me.

You're putting on this bloody turn because you think I'll blurt out something if I can be made to lose my temper. Rule number something-or-other for detectives: If they're stupid, rile them, and they'll come clean. Isn't that it? I'd have nothing against it in an up-and-coming police sergeant from the village. But from a Sir Tom-noddy, nicely grey at the well-groomed temples, and turning up just in time to be in on that Madeira, I call it a bit steep.'

'I see your point.' Appleby was looking at young Peter with what might have been called new eyes. The remarks offered to him were not merely appallingly just; they were crisply phrased. Peter Binns no doubt remained an unsatisfactory character. But it seemed very possible that Appleby had got his I.Q. quite wrong. And this decidedly didn't make him the less worthy of study. 'I see your point,' Appleby repeated. 'But the thing does work, wouldn't you admit? You are – aren't you? prodded into speaking out? We're almost within hail of understanding each other.'

'This is all rot – shooting those bloody harmless birds.' Peter had leant his gun against a tree as he thus went off at a tangent. 'Every now and then Uncle Bertram – we call him that – gets in a lot of bloodthirsty old gents who go banging away at the creatures. It's considered virtuous. Carrion crows, too. What rubbish! Do you remember getting at me about being the young squire? And how I responded like an absolute sucker? Christ! It makes me sick.'

'Then what are you doing here?'

'I got into the habit. And I got into the habit because I hadn't the guts for a clean – ' Peter checked himself, and his intermittent look of panic returned. 'Your technique works, all right,' he said sullenly.

'Clean break, Mr Binns? Or clean sweep?'

'You don't miss a trick, do you? The retired high-grade professional, still with all his old cunning at his command.

Why can't you apply it, damn you, the right way on?'

'I'm not sure that I quite follow that.'

'Didn't you say I was talking sense when I said that here was a perfectly commonplace crime? It's true that this old man had just returned to England. But there's no more than mere coincidence in that. He's old and unprotected and in a lonely place. And some thug bashes him in order to take his petty cash.'

'There's no evidence of that. But something *was* taken. You remember that Crabtree once made you a sledge. Did he make other things too? Model yachts, say? Was he a bit of a craftsman in that way?'

Peter Binns stared.

'Yes, he was. But you're merely confusing the matter again. It's miles less likely that Crabtree was killed by the sort of people who *don't* go about killing people, than that he was killed by the sort of people who *do*. That's not terribly elegant English, but I expect you see what I mean.'

'Yes, I do.'

'Then why not start at the right end? Why not go after whatever tramps and vagrants are around? Why come bothering us?'

'I'm quite sure that the local police can be trusted to go after the tramps and vagrants.'

'That's no answer. And barging in like this on any household is a damned irresponsible thing.'

'No, Mr Binns – not irresponsible. A responsibility – yes. You mean – don't you? – that when a strong wind of inquiry happens to blow through any respectable family the skeletons are likely to begin rattling in the cupboards.'

'Yes, that's what I mean. And it's unfair. The Coulsons are decent people. Daphne's all right – although I tell her she's a ghastly little bitch. My father – who, you say, was down here yesterday – is just an ordinary worried sort of father, I'd suppose. I'm not a totally hopeless little cad myself. But everybody's got *something*. Don't you see?'

'Yes, I do see. But the question, Mr Binns, is whether one of you has something that somehow hitches on to Seth Crabtree. I have no interest in any of you, apart from that.'

'But you might have.' Peter Binns was obstinate. 'You might, while looking for a crime that isn't there, hit on quite a different crime that is. What then?'

'Ah – what then.' Appleby looked at the young man curiously, and didn't for a moment reply. It was a real question, and he rather respected the boy for coming out with it. When he spoke, it was gravely. 'That would depend, you know, on the size of the crime. On its gravity.'

'But that's not very logical, is it, in a policeman?'

'No, Mr Binns, it isn't logical – or even consonant with one's responsibilities under the law. But I give you my word that it represents my own attitude.'

'I see. But what you grub up with your snooping mayn't be crime at all. It may merely be scandal, mayn't it? Just pain and humiliation and hurts that can't be mended.'

'I'm afraid that that's true.' Appleby's glance at Peter Binns was now of real surprise. For the boy was talking from some depth of feeling that one wouldn't have suspected in him.

'Or both.' Peter picked up his gun again. 'Petty crime here and deep scandal there. A mess all round. And just because this old idiot got himself killed at our back door.'

'I repeat that I see your point. But does it occur to you that you are presenting rather a lurid picture of Scroop House? More skeletons in the cupboards than it's natural to suppose would have accumulated since a mere 1786?'

'1786?' For a moment Peter Binns was at a loss. Then, for the first time, something like the flicker of a smile appeared on his face. 'You don't know us,' he said. 'And, although you're so bloody clever, there's still a chance you never will.'

'That's true enough.' Appleby nodded soberly. 'It will be a matter of – well, of the fortune of war.'

Chapter Ten

When Appleby got back to the terrace, he found it occupied only by Hollywood. The butler greeted him with respectful indifference.

'Mr Coulson and Lady Appleby have walked over to the farm, sir. Lady Appleby expressed an interest in the milking parlour. I am to direct you there, if I may.'

'Ah, yes. And Mrs Coulson?' Appleby thought that this was the point at which he might take leave of his hostess.

'Mrs Coulson has unfortunately been taken a little unwell, and has had to retire. She wished me to give you her apologies.'

'I am very sorry. Now, if you will just point out the direction of the home farm, I shall find it easily enough.'

'Yes, sir. But I had better guide you through the gardens. It is the quicker route. If you will come this way.'

Appleby, being thus constrained to Hollywood's society, judged that he might as well try to improve the occasion.

'I have been thinking,' he said, 'of what you told me – or didn't tell me – about your recollections of Crabtree.'

'Indeed, sir?'

'The question in my mind is really this: were you quite frank in the matter? Don't, please, misunderstand me. One who has been long in your responsible position in a household like this – particularly a household such as the former Mrs Coulson's was – naturally develops a good deal of reticence, particularly in the presence of strangers. That is entirely proper.'

Hollywood gave his remote bow in acknowledgement of this civil speech. He was a chilly person. Appleby wondered whether, if Tarbox's account of his vicious past were true, he had commonly begun by freezing the young persons he proposed to ravish.

'It may be so, sir. Down these steps, if you please.'

'Nothing impairs the good order of such a household more than its mistress's making an injudicious favourite or confidant of somebody with very little standing in it.'

Hollywood said nothing. He merely opened a gate and stood aside for Appleby to pass through. Appleby did so – and came firmly to a halt.

'Mr Hollywood, just what was this threat that you supposed Crabtree to be turning up with?'

'I spoke only of a very vague impression, sir.'

'You don't strike me as being a vague person. I think there was something definite in your mind. Aren't you being secretive?'

'The word is an interesting one, sir. In the connexion we are considering.'

Appleby in his turn said nothing. It almost looked as if Hollywood were coming unstuck.

'The late Mrs Coulson was secretive. At least in her later years, when I entered her service. And this is not itself a secret. You may have heard it. The left-hand path, sir.'

'One moment. Crabtree had some place in this secretive habit of hers?'

There was a moment's silence. For the first time, Hollywood had hesitated. He might have been regretting the course upon which he had embarked. Appleby tried prompting.

'Mrs Coulson's fondness for herbaceous borders – in which you say she relied upon Crabtree's taste – can scarcely have been a secret indulgence?'

'No, sir. The truth is that Crabtree had something else, as

117

well as skill in such matters. Although untrained, he was a good working carpenter.'

'And what was the significance of that?'

Again Hollywood took a moment to reply.

'Well, sir, it is matter upon which you are bound to come. It was gossiped about. The present Scroop is not an ancient house – not as the country houses of the older gentry go. But it does offer scope. It is extensive.'

'Scope?'

'For hiding things away, sir. This became something of a mania with the late Mrs Coulson. Crabtree constructed hiding-places.'

Appleby took time to digest this. It certainly opened up surprising possibilities.

'And you connect this,' he asked, 'with a certain sense of threat in Crabtree's bearing when he presented himself yesterday?'

'It is a possible line of thought, sir.'

'Mr Coulson appears to have been aware of nothing of the sort. So if Crabtree did arrive armed with some dangerous knowledge and the disposition to use it, Mr Coulson himself was not the object of his designs.'

'It may be so, sir. There are other possibilities, no doubt.'

'Quite so. We all have pasts, have we not?'

If this in any way went home to the conscience of Hollywood, he gave no sign of it – or no sign, perhaps, other than a further drop in the temperature of the chill air he seemed to inhabit.

'Yes, sir. But pasts, in the sense you suggest, cannot be hidden away in small cupboards. Only physical objects can be so hidden.'

'That's very true. Small objects in small cupboards, and large objects in large ones. For that matter, middling objects in middling ones. I've known a human body hidden in a surprisingly modest cupboard.'

This bizarre remark at least had some effect, since it caused a flicker of unidentifiable emotion to pass over the impassive features of Hollywood.

'No doubt, sir. But not, I hope, in a good family. One associates crimes and expedients of that order with the lower classes, does one not?'

Appleby found himself wondering whether, in former years, Colonel Raven's Tarbox had associated a little more with Mrs Coulson's Hollywood than he was now disposed to admit. Hollywood, when forced or persuaded to utter, discovered a rather similar vein of formal speech.

'Do I understand,' Appleby asked, 'that Crabtree actually constructed a number of small hiding-places for Mrs Coulson's use? Behind panels and under floors – that sort of thing?'

'Gossip said so, sir.'

'But what about your own certain knowledge? After all, you had the freedom of the whole house. Could you lead me – or lead your employer – to one of these supposed hiding-places now?'

For a fraction of a second Hollywood hesitated, so that Appleby had a sudden sharp sense of the man as choosing between two answers one of which, in the nature of the case, must be a flat lie.

'No, sir. Certainly not. I speak of gossip, and have perhaps been wrong to do so. But, naturally, I am anxious to help the law. You must understand that Mrs Coulson's private apartments were not always accessible to me. Again, there were occasions upon which the house was closed and the servants put upon board wages. Crabtree may have had the run of the place then.'

'I see. And what do you suppose that Mrs Coulson – the

former Mrs Coulson – was disposed to hide in these places?'

'I have never conjectured, sir. It was not my place.'

'Rubbish, man!' Appleby was suddenly briskly impatient. 'You must have thought about it, even if you didn't discuss it with others.'

'It may be so, sir.'

'Well – what was your guess?'

'I had thought of improper books, sir.'

'Had you, indeed?' Appleby found that he couldn't at all decide whether this strange suggestion proceeded from nastiness of mind or from covert mockery. 'But Crabtree could hardly have hoped to make much capital, after all those years, out of a minor depravity of that sort?'

'One would suppose not, sir. But the present Mr Coulson is a man very jealous of the honour of his family.'

'So he is.' Appleby was rather struck by the cogency of this.

'And I have thought of stolen property, to which the same consideration would apply. It is said that persons of substance, and particularly ladies, are sometimes given to petty theft in a quite irrational way. There is a word for it.'

'Kleptomania, I suppose.'

'Thank you, sir. And stolen property, if retained, must be secreted.'

'Certainly it must. But were you, in fact, ever aware of Mrs Coulson's stealing anything from anybody?'

'Dear me, no, sir. I could scarcely have remained in her employment, if I had become aware of anything of the sort. It would have been injudicious. Where mysterious disappearances occur, it is servants that commonly get the blame of it. These are only conjectures that I have been putting forward. I fear I may have been talking at random, sir.'

'I don't think so.' Appleby turned to look keenly at Hollywood. 'No – I don't think so, at all.'

'Thank you, sir. And the farm is now in front of you.'

Hollywood gave his little bow. The effect was rather as of a refrigerator taking a sudden kink in the middle. He turned and walked away.

It proved unnecessary to explore the farmyard. Bertram Coulson and Judith emerged from it just as Appleby approached.

'I'm so sorry that my wife has had to go and lie down,' Coulson said. 'She suffers from a slight migraine from time to time, but fortunately it never stays for long. She was most anxious that you should stay to lunch. I hope you will. Daphne will preside, if Edith is still on the sick-list.'

The Applebys excused themselves in proper form.

'Then you must come another day. And I hope Lady Appleby has enjoyed looking over the old place as much as I have enjoyed showing it to her. She will have seen that I am absurdly fond of Scroop. It must be partly because it came to me so unexpectedly.'

'You weren't the evident heir?' Appleby looked curiously at his host. Coulson was speaking not quite spontaneously. It was as if he has resolved upon steering the remainder of the conversation upon a determined course. He could be felt as a man anxious to get something off his chest.

'There was no very evident heir. And Sara Coulson – although, of course, not herself a Coulson – had the entire property at her disposal. It was a slightly unusual situation, in the case of a place like this – wouldn't you say? I think the county felt it to be so. Yes, I think they did.'

Appleby found himself doubting whether the county had much bothered in the matter. But it was evident that, from the first, Bertram Coulson had seen himself as very much in the eye of the gentry to whom he had been recruited.

'Was there anybody else who might have inherited?' Judith asked.

'Yes, indeed. There was my cousin Miles. A younger man – and, of course, one of the English Coulsons. Old Sara was thought to be very fond of him. But her choice fell on me.'

'And what happened to Miles?' Judith asked. 'Is he still alive?'

'Alive?' Bertram Coulson seemed startled. 'Dear me, yes. A younger man, as I said.'

'He used to come and stay here in the old lady's time?'

'Indeed he did. So what actually happened was a disappointment to him, I'm afraid.'

'Did he survive it?' Judith continued to speak rather lightly. 'I mean, has he got on all right in the world, in spite of not having become a landowner?'

'I'm afraid not.' Bertram Coulson now spoke slowly and as if with reluctance. 'Miles hasn't, I'm afraid, made much of a job of life.'

Appleby took this up.

'Which probably means, doesn't it, that he wouldn't have made much of a job of Scroop? I suspect that old Mrs Coulson was chiefly anxious about the future of the place, and made her choice in the light of that anxiety. She looked round among the surviving Coulsons in search of the competent man for the job.'

'I've certainly never managed to think of it in that light.' Bertram Coulson had flushed faintly. 'And she knew me merely by repute. But at least I've tried not to let the place down.'

For some paces the Applebys walked with their host in silence.

'I ought to tell you,' Appleby said suddenly, 'that I've had some rather curious talk with your butler. As a policeman, you understand, and not as your guest. Once more, you must forgive the awkwardness.'

'Not a bit. You know I'm only anxious to see that sad business cleared up. If any of my people can help you, they must.'

'Thank you. Hollywood's story is a very odd one. And it convicts him of having been disingenuous when he declared that old Mrs Coulson prized Crabtree simply because he had some taste in gardens. The story is that Crabtree was a good enough carpenter to contrive various hiding-places about Scroop and that in these Mrs Coulson secreted things in some more or less pathological way.'

'Hollywood came out with that?' Coulson was clearly startled. 'How extremely odd!'

'It's entirely news to you?'

Coulson made no immediate reply – perhaps because, with no great appropriateness to the moment, he had been suddenly prompted to offer Judith a cigarette.

'Hollywood,' Appleby went on, 'has no positive evidence of his own to offer. He speaks simply of gossip in Mrs Coulson's last years. Perhaps it had died away before you came to live here?'

'Yes – no.' Coulson was perplexed and almost confused. 'Gossip – perhaps. Of the old lady's secreting things. But not this of Crabtree's helping. That, no.'

'It seems to be Hollywood's view that Crabtree, when he turned up yesterday, was thinking to profit in some way from this ancient business of these hiding-places.'

'How extraordinary! How extraordinary that Hollywood should come out with such ideas!' Whether it was precisely by this thought or not, Bertram Coulson was unmistakably upset. 'It's true, of course, that in her last years the old lady

123

had her eccentric side. And there was the mystery of the money. That does look as if it might fit.'

'The money?' Appleby asked.

'More than £2,000. It was a little awkward because of probate and death-duties and so on. Of course this was a large household in those days. But it was a larger sum than one might have expected to disappear without record in so short a time.'

'Just how did it disappear?'

'I'm sorry. I'm not being at all lucid.' Coulson was still disturbed. 'During the last months of her life, Sara drew this large sum in cash from her bank. Not at one go, I believe, but in a number of smaller sums. And at her death there was no trace of it. Her solicitors, I gathered, were a good deal worried. They had a notion that it might in some way have been extorted from her – even, perhaps, by way of blackmail. That, of course, was absurd. She was a high-minded woman of the most unblemished character. But certainly touched, in those last months, by the beginnings of a senile dementia. She might have given the money away very irresponsibly. In the end it was decided that we had better be content with the supposition that she had managed to make some large charitable disbursements in cash. The sum was just not so big that it need really be a matter of large anxiety. But what if it ties up with this strange story of Hollywood's? What if Sara had turned at the end into a real miser, and had Crabtree fix her up a cache for all that money?' Coulson turned to Appleby. 'Would that fit?'

'It would fit better than some of Hollywood's notions of what the old lady might have been concerned to conceal. But it doesn't fit with the notion that, yesterday, Crabtree turned up here with something like blackmail in his head.'

'But that's nonsense, anyway!' Coulson was impatient. 'Whatever notion Hollywood may have formed, the old fellow wasn't like that in the least. I'm not an idiot, Appleby. And I can't be mistaken there.'

'Very well. Suppose that Crabtree knew of £2,000 in cash hidden somewhere in your house. He might be proposing simply to tell you about it – with or without some notion of a reward. Alternatively, he might be proposing to gain access to Scroop and quietly make off with it. But, in that case, why didn't he do so in the years that he was employed here after old Mrs Coulson's death? Had he turned less honest in old age? Had his imagination – out there in America – played more and more upon this hidden hoard until he had resolved to go for it? It's a possibility. But there's a lot that it doesn't explain.'

'It doesn't,' Judith interposed, 'explain his death. Or does it?'

'Some additional facts might. Suppose that somebody else had known about the hiding-place – and had rifled it already. And suppose Crabtree to know who that person must be. There might be a motive of sorts there for killing the old man. But we don't really want suppositions. We want a few more hard facts.'

'Quite so.' Bertram Coulson nodded. 'And I can't help hoping –with all respect to you, Appleby – that by this time that excellent fellow Hilliard has found them. Simply by following up whatever suspicious characters may have been wandering casually through this countryside yesterday.'

'And with a disposition to take a swipe at a defenceless old stranger, on the off chance of his having a few pounds in his pocket? Well, that's been in our minds before.' Appleby paused. 'And I share your hope. It might save quite a lot of trouble.' He smiled at Coulson. 'Including hunting Scroop for those hiding-places.'

'I don't think I'd mind that.'

'Perhaps not. But I've been in this sort of business for a

long time, Coulson. And I know that one hidden thing has a nasty trick of leading to another.'

Having taken their leave, the Applebys walked for some way in silence across the park.

'Wasn't that,' Judith asked, 'rather a stiff crack you took at him at the end?'

'I simply meant what I said. One digs up the relevant horror only by disinterring a lot of irrelevant ones as well. You know that. It's something I assure you of to the point of boredom.'

'All sorts of thronging horrors among the respectable landed gentry? Skeletons swinging on every family tree? You've been reading too much Ivy Compton-Burnett. Do you think, to begin with, that Bertram Coulson has some dark past?'

'I'm not sure that Hollywood wasn't going obliquely about putting something of the sort in my head. I suspect that he was providing what you might call the *one* two, knowing that I'd presently come upon the *other* two to put it together with. A deep one, is Hollywood.'

'Aren't you convinced that they're all deep ones in this affair?'

'Yes, I am – absolutely.'

'Well, that's candid, at least. But go back to this nice Bertram Coulson, who's had all that difficulty in persuading himself that he's adequate in the role of a perfectly ordinary country gentleman. Do you think he has some frightful past?'

'I think he may have a frightful future.'

'Don't be tiresome, John.'

'Well, at the lowest he's a man beset by some very queer doubt. And it can't simply be, "Am I really like the dear old squire?" There may be a small element in the man of something of that order. Because he isn't one of the English Coulsons, and so forth. But he's had the same sort of breeding as the folk he calls "the county" – or as near as makes no difference. So the thing doesn't make sense. No – if he's a man in some way undermined, it's by a doubt of some quite different quality.'

'Might it be a doubt about his wife? Remember Uncle Julius's queer impression of her.'

'I remember my own impression.' Appleby spoke soberly. 'A good sort of woman, I thought. But I did find myself thinking other things as well. What's the house like, by the way? William Chambers going strong?'

Judith nodded.

'Rather lovely,' she said. 'The *chinoiseries* aren't quite up to a tiptop place like Claydon, say. But they're pretty good. And Bertram is terribly proud of everything. Yet it's a mix-up, in a way, rather as *he* is. Half a dozen rather good eighteenth-century paintings and a really fine range of the water-colourists. But two or three modish modern things he's obviously been told indicate enlightened patronage today. Some superb French pieces, but even more ultra-shiny, high-grade reproduction antique. A gunroom with far too many guns. The wrong sort of dogs – ' Judith broke off in high indignation as her husband suddenly shouted with laughter. 'Of course if you won't be *serious* – ' she began.

'Perhaps it *is* impossible for a mere colonial gent to become an English one. Too many guns – what a solecism! Pug dogs – '

'Of course they're not – '

'Or at least dogs that are almost human. How very shocking! Damme, sir, the fellow's a mere counter-jumper. Cockney accent, too. Comes from Australia, they say. Calls himself a Coulson, and I suppose he was vetted by the old gel – Sara, did they call her? – who was straight out of the right stable, bless her. But there's a touch of convict blood in this fellow, if you ask me.'

'Don't be a buffoon.' Judith, with some satisfaction, continued to be furious. 'You remind me of that odious Channing-Kennedy.'

'Ah – Channing-Kennedy.' Appleby was suddenly completely serious. 'Judith – I wonder whether, perhaps, it's rather useful to be reminded of him?'

Chapter Eleven

'Of course, they're a philistine crowd round here.'

Colonel Julius Raven pronounced this judgement as he stood before his sideboard and carved, with a connoisseur's care, a choice chunk of cold salmon for his niece. Although himself a soldier and of simple mind, he was the head of a family so prolific in poets, painters, sculptors, scholars and madmen generally that he was thus prompted at times to speak of his rural neighbours with this sort of benevolent condescension.

'Even at Scroop?' Judith asked.

'Oh, dear me, yes. Bertram Coulson is all piety, as you've seen. But he wouldn't have cut much of a figure among the Souls, and all that lot. Arthur Balfour, now. I never did much care for that fellow. All intellect and sensibility and amateur professor on the one hand. But look at his handling of Ireland on the other.' Colonel Raven had one of his vague moments. 'My dear, what am I talking about?'

'The people at Scroop.'

'Ah, yes. Betram Coulson must be a man of ability, you know. Mayonnaise? I don't recommend it. Tea-shop stuff at the best, if you ask me. Small drop of vinegar?'

'Small drop of vinegar, Uncle Julius.'

'Vinegar? A very good idea. Excellent. I'm delighted you thought of it, my dear. Now, what was I saying? Ah, yes. Young Coulson at Scroop. Able man. Stands to reason. Cattle in a big way in the colonies, and so forth. But only the local backwoodsmen visit at Scroop. Decent fellows and all that. But no brains, bless them. No taste, if the truth be told. Not as in the old girl's time. Lion and the lizard, don't you know. Haunting the courts where the other fellow had cut rather a figure. Good poem. Loaf of bread beneath the bough. Drop of hock? Only thing I ever touch in the middle of the day. Should be almost frozen, and then allowed to return to cellar temperature. Something that that dunderhead Tarbox discovered. Clever chap.'

'Uncle Julius, do you know anything about Miles Coulson?'

'Miles?' Colonel Raven looked seriously at his niece and shook his head. 'He used to be there quite a lot. Had an odd profession for a Coulson. Ominous, you might say, from the start. A mummer.'

'Miles Coulson was an actor?'

'Actor?' Colonel Raven appeared to have difficulty in placing this word. 'Quite correct, my dear. Stage player. Talented, I've been told. And, of course, old Sara had all sorts round the place. Hicks. And the fat fellow who was in *Chu Chin Chow*. Anyone at his own particular top. So Miles would usually have some of his own kidney.'

'There was some idea that this Miles Coulson might inherit the place?'

'Yes, I believe so. But it didn't happen that way. Perhaps the old girl found out something to his discredit. Or perhaps she simply preferred the sound of Bertram Coulson, out in the antipodes with all those wholesome sheep and cattle. And Miles may have taken it a little hard.'

'What does Miles do now?'

'I've no idea, my dear. I've never heard him mentioned for years. Went off the rails, they say. But I don't know how badly. Sad thing, when a decent family produces a rotter. Came across it once or twice in the Regiment. Honoured name, you know. And then suddenly you have a boy forging a cheque or cheating at cards. Embarrassing.' For a moment

Colonel Raven looked extremely serious. Then he brightened. 'But I see that Tarbox has let us have the Stilton,' he said. 'Dig into it, John. It's really not bad – not as Stilton goes nowadays.'

Appleby did as he was bidden.

'No – no more hock, thank you,' he said. 'We had to drink a glass of Madeira with the Coulsons. Something Bertram Coulson had read about in a book, I felt. But I judged him an interesting chap. He took Judith over the house.'

'And his wife?'

'Well – an interesting woman.' Appleby smiled. 'But she went on sick parade half-way through our call.'

'Did she, indeed?' Colonel Raven sounded concerned. 'Would you say, John, that she seemed to have had a shock?'

'Well, yes. I think that the death of this old man so close by had affected her.'

'The death of an old man?' For a short but unmistakable moment, Colonel Raven was quite at sea. 'Ah, Crabtree,' he then said. 'Yes, of course.'

Appleby looked curiously at his host.

'It was something else you had in mind?'

'Oh, no. Oh, dear me, no. Stilton, Judith? Or there's this Italian stuff, if your taste lies that way.'

Judith took some of the Italian stuff. And at Colonel Raven's board there was a silence of a totally unfamiliar sort. For – incredibly – Colonel Raven had somehow failed in candour. He had even given his niece and her husband what could only be called a furtive look. The thing was as astounding as if he had himself produced a pack of cards with six aces. Appleby knew that he had to speak. But he found himself taking a deep breath before doing so.

'Colonel – you remember our talk about the Coulsons at dinner last night?'

'About the Coulsons?' Colonel Raven repeated the name

with a vagueness that seemed in part genuine and in part an embarrassing continuation of his sudden odd behaviour. 'Ah, yes – we talked about them, of course.'

'You said something about Mrs Coulson that you were then reluctant to enlarge on or even to stand by. Not exactly about her moral character, but about – well, perhaps her disposition in that general area of conduct.'

'Did I, my dear John? I'm sorry to hear it. Comes of neglecting the drill, wouldn't you say? Never knew a decent Mess where a fellow was allowed to name a lady at dinner.'

'No doubt.' Appleby didn't wholly manage to exclude a certain impatience from his reception of this. 'But what I want to know, Colonel, is this: was there anything in the recent past that prompted you to that particular line of comment on Mrs Coulson?'

'Really, John, I don't, if I may say so, care for this at all. My fault, clearly. Talking out of turn in the most shocking way. Can I have had a glass too much of that burgundy, would you say? But I think we'll drop the subject, if you don't mind.'

'But I do mind.' Appleby was inexorable. 'I repeat my question. Have you, just lately, come upon Mrs Coulson in any relation or situation that might have prompted what slipped from you about her last night?'

'My dear John, you surprise me.' The Colonel said this in evident distress. At the same time he got to his feet with a decision that somehow suggested a very senior man's severe rebuke. 'Coffee will be in the library, I think.'

'But please consider, sir.' Appleby sat tight. Judith, he saw, was watching this unexpected collision with detached interest. 'My question might not, in normal circumstances, be one which it would be decent to press if you considered it improper. But remember its present context. A context of murder. Flat murder. Make no mistake about that. Has Seth Crabtree gone out of your head?'

'Crabtree?' From being severe, Colonel Raven appeared to have relapsed upon being confused. 'Of course I haven't forgotten Crabtree. Crabtree may have been the figure that I – ' He checked himself, stiffened, and then spoke with an entirely regained composure. 'It won't do, John. There are things a gentleman doesn't tell.'

Appleby again felt himself taking a deep breath. A gentleman, he was thinking, had to be both a gentleman and in his later seventies in order to speak about a gentleman in quite this grand manner. And certainly Colonel Raven didn't make a habit of it. He had said something which he might live to be ninety without ever saying again.

'Thank you,' Appleby said. He gave Judith a glance which was a serio-comic acknowledgement of defeat. 'And coffee in the library, of course.'

'He routed you,' Judith said with mild malice, as they took an afternoon walk. 'Uncle Julius routed you. You were enjoying the Stilton. But you left a chunk of it on your plate.'

'You always were observant in these small domestic matters.' Appleby paused to light his pipe. 'But did you keep your eye on your uncle as well? What was our little *contretemps* all about?'

'It was about being a gentleman.'

'Yes, I rather gathered that. What gentlemen do do, and what they don't do. They may say something about a woman being a bit of a girl, but will draw back from anything one might call an actual aspersion on her character. We had all that last night. Today we had something further and different. A gentleman won't tell of seeing something it wasn't his business to see. Even if it was something that ended in murder.'

Judith was startled.

'John, you're letting your imagination run away with you. Uncle Julius has no notion of anything he may have seen as ending in murder. He doesn't, for one thing, put two and two together all that quickly. Not now. He sees one thing at a time. I think he saw Mrs Coulson – perhaps actually yesterday – in what he judged was a compromising situation. And that prompted him to speak rather unguardedly last night. But actual telling tales is something he's incapable of – even with a top policeman booming away at him over his own table about a context of murder. That's all.'

'I admit the booming.' It wasn't wholly amiably that Appleby did this. 'As to its being all – well, I hope it is. Do you remember that, earlier today, you were wondering whether it was perhaps your uncle who had killed Crabtree? I wasn't very sympathetic to the speculation. It seemed an example of a peculiar sense of humour that comes over you from time to time.'

'Did it, indeed. Well?'

'Your idea was, I think, that your uncle had taken a sudden swipe at Crabtree because he remembered him as a damned scoundrel of a poacher. I thought it implausible. But I'm more prepared to entertain the notion of Uncle Julius as a homicide now.'

'John!' Judith had stopped in her tracks. She was really alarmed. 'Are you serious?'

'I haven't said anything very positive, you know. Your uncle still lies well back in the race. It's just that he's put on a bit of a spurt since lunch.'

'I'd like to know how.'

'Very well. Can you imagine Mrs Coulson – the present Mrs Coulson – as keeping what they call an assignation?'

'An assignation?' Judith considered this seriously. 'Yes, I can. With a very young man.'

'A very *young* man?' Appleby frowned. 'Are you sure?'

'Yes. I'm sure. But only as the likeliest thing. Women of that age and with that temperment and in that situation – '

'That situation?'

'Mildly disillusioned as wives and very much deprived as not being mothers. It's very young men they usually fall for. Maternal mistresses. And sometimes with a terrible passion.'

'In which case it works?'

'In a way. And for a time. It may end in tragedy but it hasn't been merely a mess. Because something that's really there has, after a fashion, been satisfied.'

'Say, Mrs Coulson and Peter Binns?'

'In theory, yes.' Judith was frowning. 'But I doubt whether women often become the maternal mistresses of boys they've really *mothered*.' She shook her head. 'It's an idea. Not one I'd thought of. Not one I like.'

'What about a mature man?'

'A middle-aged man? Of course that happens too. But there's a higher proportion of mess and a quicker disillusionment.' Judith paused to look about her. 'Where are we going, John?'

'Just for a stroll. Say four miles there and four miles back. Say to the tunnel. And the Jolly Leggers.'

'I see.' Judith glanced curiously at her husband. 'Am I right?'

'In all that psychology of sex? Absolutely. It holds from *Le Rouge et le Noir* to Havelock Ellis.'

'I'd have thought it might hold a bit beyond poor old Havelock Ellis. He's a terrible antique.'

'Is he? Let's talk sense.' Appleby's pipe had gone out, and he stopped to light it again. 'We have a general situation. Edith Coulson – isn't that her name? – keeping an assignation with a lover, or with some postulant for that position.

A younger man turned to in passion, or an older man turned to in muddle. We don't know. But suppose something of the sort. And then suppose a peeping Tom.'

'John, you have the most revolting notions.'

'Suppose even a peeping Tom who shows some disposition to be a blackmailer as well. And then suppose your Uncle Julius coming on the scene. What would he do?'

Judith had gone pale.

'Hit out.'

'Very conceivably that. Which is why I say that he has put on a spurt.' Appleby paused. 'What do you think of that?'

'I think it's about as nasty an explanation of the Crabtree affair as can be conceived.'

'If a way to the better there be, it exacts a full look at the worst.'

Judith stopped and stared.

'Is that more Kipling, John?'

'No. It's Thomas Hardy. And it makes quite good policeman's sense. If you're going to find a really satisfactory solution to a problem, you'd better consider all the unsatisfactory ones in turn. None of them may be right, but they may all contribute something. Play around with this general notion of Mrs Coulson, a lover, Crabtree and your uncle, and – well, something may click into place.'

'I see.' Judith shook her head with something less than her usual satisfaction in facing up to things. 'You know, it's all not very nice.'

'That's true, I'm afraid. And – do you know? – talking of things that aren't very nice, I think we might pay a call on our friend at the Jolly Leggers.'

'That awful Channing-Kennedy? He can't really be involved, can he?'

'You might call him a contact. The dead man – I mean,

the dead man to be – swam into our ken when emerging from his pub.'

'And was being spied on there, too.'

'Precisely. I think we'd better say that Channing-Kennedy deserves a visit.'

The tunnel yawned as it had yawned before. Appleby paused to stare at it.

'Symbolical, wouldn't you say?' he asked Judith. 'All that classical ornament – just like the exterior decorum and seemliness of Scroop House. But framing darkness and mystery. And daylight perhaps a long way ahead.'

'You mean this Crabtree business may go on and on? I don't think that's a good idea, at all. Clear it up, for goodness sake, and let's spend the rest of our time down here in a reasonable way. Getting a few decent walks, and drinking that burgundy without peeping over the wine-glass to decide whether Uncle Julius is a homicidal maniac.'

'Very well, my dear.' If Appleby regarded these as highly irrational remarks on Judith's part, he didn't show it. 'Will you give me till midnight?'

'Certainly – and to the last stroke of the hour.'

'Very well. And meantime we'll go into the pub. But the bar won't be open. Shall we ask Channing-Kennedy to give us tea?'

'What you'll have to ask him, I suppose, is whether he had any actual communication with Crabtree.'

'Exactly. But we'll do it over his toasted tea-cake. Come along.'

Mr Channing-Kennedy, although he must have remembered the Applebys as a not wholly sympathetic pair, was entirely willing to hover over the fare his hostelry was able to provide.

'Delighted to see you again,' he said. 'I gather you're staying in the district. Raven Park – eh? Old Colonel Pryde. Fine place. Splendid old aristocratic type.'

'Colonel Raven,' Judith said. 'Pryde Park.' She offered these corrections as nicely as she could. John, presumably, was anxious that Channing-Kennedy should produce a vein of relaxed talk.

'Quite so. I haven't, as a matter of fact, had the pleasure of meeting the Colonel. When I came down here, no end of chaps wanted to give me introductions to one local family or another. But I was never one to push. Channing-Kennedys have never pushed. Had no need to, to be quite frank. Have our own little niche, you know.' He turned to Appleby. 'Acquainted with Herefordshire?'

'Hardly at all.'

'In Herefordshire,' Channing-Kennedy said firmly, 'there's a church pretty well full of us. Elizabethan Channings in the chancel. Jacobean Kennedys in the aisles. Eighteenth-century Channing-Kennedys in the – um . . .' The landlord of the Jolly Leggers appeared momentarily at a loss.

'Transepts?' Judith suggested.

'Just that. Army, Navy, Bar, Church – the whole thing. Sobering. Makes a fellow feel he has something to live up to – eh?'

'Yes, it must do.' Judith wondered whether the present Channing-Kennedy had to keep his end up too, as the last of a long line of pathological liars. 'And you were in the Army yourself?'

'Not the Army. The dear old R.A.F. Couple of crates pretty well shot away from under me – I don't mind telling you – and twice in the big drink. Ah, those were the days!'

'I'm afraid you must find it a dull life down here, Mr

138

Channing-Kennedy. But there was rather a grim piece of excitement yesterday, wasn't there?'

'Excitement?' For a moment Channing-Kennedy looked blank. 'Oh, you mean the old fellow who was drowned. I can't say it pushed up my pulse-rate, you know.' The landlord of the Jolly Leggers gave his sudden bellow of unbeautiful laughter. Then he looked guardedly round the little lounge in which tea had been provided. It was deserted. 'I don't know whether you've heard any talk,' he said. 'But the police are interested. They suspect foul play. And it wouldn't surprise me if they turned out to be right.'

Appleby put down his tea-cup.

'You mean,' he asked, 'that you have some evidence which would support that view?'

'Well, it was coming to him, if you ask me. Not, mind you, that I know anything about him, or as much as what his name was. I'd never set eyes on him until the evening before last. He came into the public bar not long after opening time, and he was there when I went in to relieve my barman. He'd had a pint or two over the mark, I saw at once, and I made up my mind he wasn't going to have any more. One can't expect, you know, to pull up a place like this, if one allows any trouble in the public.'

'I suppose not. But do you mean that this old man was being rowdy or quarrelsome?'

'Threatening. That would be the word.'

'But it doesn't sound at all like him.' Judith struck in with this. 'We talked to him, you see – here, outside the inn – yesterday. He seemed rather a gentle person.'

'Ah, you never know them – not till they're in liquor. Not that class.' Channing-Kennedy shook his head – a gentleman whose modest means of livelihood constrained him to a wide knowledge of the lower orders. 'They can't hold it, you know. Not like you and me.'

'Just whom was Crabtree threatening?' Appleby asked.

'Crabtree?'

'That was his name. I'd have thought you might have heard it by this time. Was he threatening somebody in the bar?'

'Not exactly that. He was arguing with some yokel about the past in these parts. I have a notion he was native here but had only just returned. And he was claiming some sort of consequence about the place in golden times gone by. That sort of thing. I was too busy with a brisk trade to pay much attention to him. And that reminds me.' Channing-Kennedy, who had sat down while thus familiarly discoursing, got to his feet again. 'I've one or two things to attend to. Got a guest stopping in the inn, as a matter of fact. Turned up without notice last night. Wealthy, if you ask me. Must find a bottle of wine for his dinner. Anything more I can have them fetch you?'

'Nothing more, thank you. It's been an excellent tea.' Appleby bit with disingenuous appreciation into a small cake of displeasing antiquity. 'But you haven't told us just where the threats came in.'

'Oh, that.' Channing-Kennedy now seemed indisposed to linger. Perhaps he had recalled that the consumers of two three-and-sixpenny teas were of much less account than a wealthy resident. 'It seemed to tie up with the place you were asking me about yesterday – Scroop House, on the other side of the canal. I gathered that this old man had once been employed there. And he was proposing to turn up and be welcomed home. That sort of thing. And this yokel – '

'Whom you could identify?'

Appleby had flashed this out with a suddenness that brought Channing-Kennedy to a standstill.

'Well, no,' he said. 'Probably not. I was pretty busy, as I was saying. And all these clodhoppers look pretty much the

140

same to me. But he must have got this old Crabnose – '

'Crabtree.'

'He must have got Crabtree – who was half-seas over, as I said – pretty well riled. Because the next thing I hear the old fellow say was, that if they did him dirt at Scroop House – he could bring red ruin on the place.'

'That would be just idle talk, wouldn't it?'

'Well, old boy, I don't know that I'd care to say.' Channing-Kennedy – easy equal of all old boys, and a man of judicious mind – shook his head. 'Reported as I'm reporting it, it does sound just like that. He could dig out of Scroop, he said, what would send Bertie Coulson – '

'Bertram Coulson?'

'Perhaps so. I wasn't, as I've said, paying all that attention. He could dig up what would send some Coulson or other packing. And more talk of that sort. If he meant business, he was asking for it.'

'Asking for business?' Judith said.

Channing-Kennedy gave his coarse bellow.

'Asking to be hit on the head,' he said, 'Or hit wherever he was hit. If he was hit at all, that's to say. For I know nothing about it, as I said. And now I must be getting along. Delighted you dropped in. If you think to mention my tunnel to any of your touring friends, I'll be grateful. Perhaps I told you I want to work up a little in the tourist line? Show some decent returns to my bloody brewery, you know, and they may shunt me up their rotten little ladder. Poor sort of ambition, eh? I don't know what old Lord Gervase would have thought of it.'

'Lord Gervase?' Judith asked.

'Oh, just a great-grandfather of mine. He might think keeping a pot-house a bit off, wouldn't you say? But let's face it. Hard times these for gentlefolk, eh? Well, chin-chin.'

Chapter Twelve

The departure of Mr Channing-Kennedy was succeeded by a sober silence. However often they encountered him, Judith was thinking, he would leave this effect behind him.

'How frightful,' she presently said. 'Do we – do you and I – really consent to belong to a social system that produces such an awful little man?'

Appleby laughed. He commonly did this when Judith was surprised into admitting the horrors of English life.

'But what do you make of him?' he asked. 'Is he just a comic turn? What did you think of his story?'

'It doesn't fit the Crabtree we know.'

'Perhaps not. But it does fit some other things.'

'And he's a shocking liar. All that about Channings and Kennedys positively crowding out the living in some country church. And Lord Gervase. Nobody was ever called Lord Gervase except in a novel.'

'Do you know that you are very much given to rash generalizations? But about his being a liar. I just don't know.'

'You don't mean that you *believe* in Lord Gervase?'

'Of course not. He was telling a great many lies, I agree. But I just wonder whether his telling lies was itself a kind of lie.'

'If I go in for generalizations, John, you go in for conundrums.'

'Well now, suppose he wasn't inventing this stuff about Crabtree. Suppose that Crabtree, having got tight, did make that rash speech to some nameless rustic. And suppose yet again that, in doing so, Crabtree in his turn wasn't inventing things. How could he, if admitted to Scroop House, dig up what would send Bertram Coulson packing?'

'A will.' Judith produced this solution with a promptitude which was, perhaps, unsurprising. 'Old Mrs Coulson was undecided about an heir. Eventually she decided upon Bertram Coulson, and she fixed it up with solicitors and people in the regular way. But later, being a bit gaga, she changed her mind and settled on somebody else – probably on her earlier favourite – the one who was an actor and eventually went to the bad.'

'Miles Coulson? And then?'

'She made one of those simple wills that are perfectly valid, although done without lawyers. And she got Crabtree to construct one of his hiding-places for it. So, ever since her death, it has been in Crabtree's power to have this will unearthed, and Bertram Coulson dispossessed in favour of Miles or whoever was named in it. What do you think of that?'

'I think it suggests that the meeting of Bertram Coulson and Crabtree yesterday morning wasn't at all the kind of affair Crabtree described to us. It presents your dear old Seth, strayed out from *Under the Greenwood Tree* or wherever, as a very respectably cunning old rascal.'

'Well, yes. But then we have to consider everything. You keep on saying that. And you made quite a point of feeling or believing that Crabtree had something to conceal.'

'That's true. So Bertram Coulson killed Crabtree in order not to be turned out of Scroop House?'

'Just that.' Judith nodded gravely. 'You've seen how madly attached to the place Bertram is. He'd do anything rather than risk losing it.'

'True again. But I think there are certain difficulties which your theory must face.'

'Of course there are. I don't believe Bertram Coulson to be at all that sort of man.'

'Perhaps he's not. But there is still a difficulty, even if he is. For, whatever his moral nature, there can be no doubt of his having a reasonably good practical intelligence. He packed meat, or whatever it was, sufficiently successfully to tell us that. So he must know very well that an English landed proprietor is in singularly little danger of being deprived of his estate on the strength of a twenty-year-old will. Particularly when that will would seem to have been made by an old woman whose chief concern was to hide it away from all human ken except that of one of her menservants. No court would look seriously at a document with so daft a provenance.'

'I think I could guess that. But your argument neglects one significant – ' Judith broke off, having become aware that a stranger had entered the lounge and was making his way through it to the inn's only staircase. She waited until he had disappeared. 'I was going to say – ' But again she broke off, this time on catching sight of her husband's expression. 'My dear John, what on earth is it?'

'Am I goggling and gaping? How very unprofessional. But that was Alfred Binns, the father of your *enfants terribles*, who was so sure that he was doing no more than hurrying through this part of the country last night.'

'He must be Channing-Kennedy's wealthy guest, who's actually going to have a bottle of wine.'

'So he must. I wonder – '

This time it was Appleby who fell abruptly silent. For the figure which had disappeared upstairs was now coming down again. It was certainly Binns. And the object of his return to the lounge immediately declared itself. Without pausing at the foot of the stairs, he walked straight over to Appleby.

'Good afternoon,' he said.

'Good afternoon.' Appleby rose. 'May I introduce you to my wife?'

Alfred Binns produced a formal bow.

'How do you do?' he said. 'The fact is, Lady Appleby, that your husband and I ought to have a little conversation.'

Judith, although not precisely habituated to the role of the little woman who scurries from the room when the menfolk broach business, produced a very colourable impersonation of something of this sort now.

'I think I'll take a *teeny* toddle along the canal,' she said. 'But don't be *too* long, darling.' And with this Judith withdrew.

'Lady Appleby has a sense of humour,' Binns said. He didn't sound too pleased by the discovery.

'Well, yes – and of a freakish sort at times.'

'Perhaps I made my suggestion a little baldly, Sir John. But I do think we must talk. For your better information and for my better safety.'

'Your better safety, sir?' Appleby sat down again. 'I don't know that I follow you.'

'I doubt that. Here I am, hanging around what must be called the scene of the crime. And last night it was perfectly apparent, wasn't it, that you were listening to a pack of lies?'

'I don't know that I'd say a pack, Mr Binns. But some lies, certainly.'

'Including a big one.'

'I agree. You asserted that it was a mere matter of chance that you were in this part of the world at the time of Crabtree's death. That wasn't true.'

'Exactly. And it was an untruth in a damned dangerous area. That's what I mean by considering my own better safety now. Of course, if I'd actually killed that old man myself, I'd scarcely have barged in on Raven as I did. I'd have beaten it.'

'In that rather obvious car. Do you know that I saw the Rolls, with yourself presumably in it, within a few hundred yards of that lock and within twenty minutes, or thereabouts, of Crabtree's being killed?'

'I said we should talk.'

'We're talking. You say, or imply, that you didn't kill Crabtree. Perhaps you're afraid that one of your children did?'

The sudden brutality of this question sent the blood from Alfred Binns's face. But it produced nothing unguarded from him.

'It's certainly about my children that I want to speak, Sir John. For there is something to tell about them, as there is about myself. And, thinking over the gravity of this affair, I have seen how essential absolute candour is.'

Appleby didn't show himself as much impressed by this very proper speech.

'It is my impression,' he said, 'that you knew about what you call the gravity of this affair before you turned up upon Colonel Raven last night. Truthfully or untruthfully, you declared that you were unaware of Crabtree's death. But something had shocked you badly, all the same.'

'Crabtree's death.' Binns's voice was steady. And his gaze was steady too. 'I think I was probably the fourth person to be aware of it.'

'The *fourth* person?'

'First – necessarily – the murderer. Then you and Lady Appleby. And then myself. It seems to take some explaining, does it not?'

'It certainly does.'

'Crabtree, as you probably know, was in my employment

for a number of years during my tenancy of Scroop. Perhaps five years. Towards the end of that period I judged that he had become an undesirable influence upon my small son, Peter.'

'Gravely undesirable?'

'Yes.'

'Was this a matter of some definite depravity – say a sexual depravity?'

'Not at all. It was an indefinable influence – and only the more disturbing because of that.'

'I see. Would it have been accurate to describe Crabtree as a sinister character?'

'Again – not at all. He was an attractive man.'

'Attractive to women?'

Binns hesitated. He might have been checking a recollection.

'Yes,' he said. 'I think so. Be that as it may, I decided that we should be better without him. We parted amicably enough.'

'You dismissed him because of something ill-defined, unsubstantiated and discreditable – but he went off amicably, all the same?'

'There was no breach. I gave him a substantial sum of money to enable him to settle overseas.'

'Dear me!' Appleby looked curiously at Binns. 'You must have been uncommonly anxious to get rid of him. Looking back over the situation afterwards, did you continue to feel that your alarm about his influence over Peter had been justified?'

'I did. Naturally enough, in subsequent years Crabtree was seldom mentioned in my household. But when he was – well, there was *something*. Perhaps I express myself obscurely. My son was being reminded of something not grateful to him.'

147

'What about your daughter? Had the man had some ill influence over her?'

'Daphne?' Binns seemed startled. 'Certainly not. She can have been no more than four or five when Crabtree went abroad.'

'But a moment ago, Mr Binns, you implied that it was both your children that you wanted to speak about.'

'That, in a way, is true. Although Peter and Daphne do not always appear to get on very well, they are much in one another's confidence. The troubles of one would be the troubles of the other.'

'I see.' Appleby wasn't, in fact, sure that he did see. 'And what follows from all this? Just how does it hitch on to yesterday – and to our present conversation?'

'I had a letter from Crabtree, announcing his return to England, and saying that he expected to be at Scroop in a couple of days time.'

'Could it have been called a threatening letter?'

'I think not. Although I confess that I read into it some obscure attitude that I didn't like. I have, of course, preserved it. You can see it.'

Appleby was silent for a moment. He realized that this must be true.

'But I don't see,' he said, 'that this was any great concern of yours. Did the letter mention your son and daughter?'

'Yes. Crabtree said he hoped he would have an opportunity to see them.'

'He had known them as children. Apart from that old distrust of the man, there was really nothing to alarm you in a perfectly natural wish?'

'There ought not to have been, I agree. Perhaps I am a pathologically anxious parent. I was, in fact, alarmed – or disquieted, at least.'

'Where were Peter and Daphne at this time?'

148

'I had understood that they were visiting an aunt in Wales. When I found that this was not the case, I guessed that they had come to Scroop. They have a standing invitation from the Coulsons. My uneasiness grew.'

'I'm bound to say I find this a little odd. But I suppose you telephoned or wired Scroop to find out?'

'No. I decided to run down. You will wonder with what object. I can only answer: reassurance. I wanted to be certain that there was not some threat to Peter in Crabtree's return.'

'After fifteen years?'

'It seems strange. But I suppose most people have these irrational impulses at times. Of course my subsequent behaviour – which is really what I have to tell you about – was more irrational still. That is the – well, the awkwardness of it. I decided not to call on the Coulsons. It is a long time since I have done so, and I felt some reluctance about renewing our acquaintance. So I decided to approach the house from across the canal and through the park. I felt I should probably see some sign of the children if they were in fact at Scroop. Does this sound incredible, Sir John?'

Appleby shook his head.

'I can't say that it does. Not, that is to say, as a course of conduct which some unknown person might adopt. It doesn't entirely, if I may say so, cohere with my sense of your own character, Mr Binns. But I have been coming across a good deal in this affair where similar considerations apply. And your plan didn't succeed?'

'I scarcely gave it a chance to. I drove along the road south of the canal, and came to a stop not far from the lock, with the plan I have mentioned to you still in my mind. Then, suddenly, I thought better of it. My children would find my visit, and the manner of my visit, strange. It was scarcely possible that Crabtree's return really constituted any threat to my son. I decided that I had been foolish, and I drove on.'

'There seems nothing very surprising in that.' Appleby said this rather drily. 'And then?'

'And then I changed my mind once more. Frankly, I was in a state of nervous irresolution. I turned round, drove back, left the car, and walked up to the lock. And there you were: yourself, Lady Appleby, and the body of Seth Crabtree. I turned and walked away again.' Binns looked at Appleby with faint amusement. 'And you didn't notice me.'

'Well, well.' Appleby was suitably abashed. 'Of course, I was preoccupied, and so was my wife. But I *had* noticed you earlier, or at least I had noticed your car. You got near enough, by the way, to recognize Crabtree – and after those fifteen years?'

'Yes . . . no.' Binns appeared honestly uncertain. 'Say that the thing flashed on me. I just knew.'

'And then?' Appleby thought he had caught a ring of truth in this. 'You drove away and thought it over? And it had been a terrific shock? And, later, all you could think of was blundering in on Colonel Raven with that story of passing through – your hope being to find out whether your children actually were at Scroop?'

'Just that, Sir John. Afterwards, I come back to this inn and put up here. I couldn't bring myself to clear out.' Binns paused, and then looked full at Appleby. 'Have you the slightest reason to believe that I am telling the truth?'

'Well – yes, I have. Or at least some of it.'

'You mean having seen my car at a time and place that fits?'

'Of course, there is that. And at a time and place, Mr Binns, that would fit with a good deal. But there's more than that. Your story has a very odd shape to it. But I can fit at least one loop of it, so to speak, into the jigsaw.'

'There is a jigsaw?' Binns spoke swiftly. 'One, I mean, that is beginning to show a pattern?'

'Dear me, yes. I've been looking into this affair, you know, for more than twenty-four hours now.'

'Yes, of course.' Alfred Binns received this sudden shocking piece of arrogance almost humbly.

'And I'm under a sort of contract, as a matter of fact, to clear it up by midnight. By the way, when your son was quite small, and when you had Crabtree about the place, was there any one thing about the boy that particularly worried you?'

Binns suddenly passed a hand rather wearily over his forehead.

'It seems strange,' he said. 'But that's just the sort of thing I can't remember.'

'For example, did the boy sometimes seem to have more pocket-money than seemed accountable?'

Alfred Binns stared.

'Why, yes,' he said. That's true. It was a worry. I used to wonder whether he was going to his mother's purse. She . . . we parted, you know, when Peter was about fifteen. But up till then.'

'I see. And later? Have there been later occasions, I mean, upon which Peter has seemed oddly flush?'

Binns frowned.

'Perhaps there have. There was his second car. It looked remarkably expensive. Peter said he'd traded in his old one in some advantageous way. But I remember feeling that there was something to account for.'

'Thank you.' Appleby nodded gravely. 'I ought to say that, in the nature of the case, your son remains just as much a suspect as you do. Rather more so, perhaps – since I could provide a motive of sorts for his killing Crabtree. I shall probably be in a position to provide one for you too. But it may take just a little thinking out. You are a slightly more mysterious figure to me, Mr Binns, than your son is. In fact,

I see nothing that is mysterious about Peter. Your daughter, however, is another matter.'

Binns had received the first part of this speech impassively. But its conclusion brought him to his feet.

'Daphne has nothing to do with this,' he said. 'She has no part in it at all. I'll thank you to leave her alone.'

'I hope I shall be able to. But has what you have told me, Mr Binns, really been entirely dictated by a sense of what you called your own better safety? Are you quite sure that Daphne's better safety hasn't been a little in the picture too?'

For a moment Binns was silent. When he spoke, it was with a sudden vehemence which bore every appearance of spontaneity.

'For God's sake,' he said, 'live up to your boasting. Find who killed Crabtree. And find him by midnight. I can't stand much more of this.'

Chapter Thirteen

Judith Appleby's teeny toddle had not, in fact, been along the canal. That – she discovered – was a route she never wanted to take again. It was the route, after all, that had led from Seth Crabtree alive and conversable to Seth Crabtree dead and battered. She had therefore turned in the other direction on leaving the inn and taken the narrow lane down which the disagreeable vanman had retreated with his rejected piano. She would explore the hamlet of Nether Scroop.

It didn't look as if this enterprise could occupy her for long. There was a small church which might, or might not be of interest; there was a village shop which was also a post-office; there was a scattering of cottages round an uncertain demarcated green; and behind hedges there were two or three houses of slightly larger pretension. Just emerging from the garden gate of one of these last was the only figure visible in the scene. It was that of a woman who, seeing Judith's approach, first hesitated and then waited for her to come up. As she did so, Judith realized that it was Mrs Coulson.

For a moment Judith couldn't recall why this encounter took her slightly by surprise. Then she remembered.

'Good afternoon,' she said. 'I'm so glad that you are better.'

'Better?' Mrs Coulson looked vague. Then she smiled. 'These small attacks never last. I was only sorry to have to go and lie down during your call.' She hesitated. 'You are looking round the village? Shall we walk together to the church? There is one rather lovely Elizabethan tomb.'

'Yes, I should like to see that.'

Mrs Coulson took a step forward. As she did so, the garden gate by which she had been standing swung to, and Judith saw that it carried a small brass plate:

BRIAN WEST M.B., B.S.
PHYSICIAN AND SURGEON

It was to be presumed that Mrs Coulson's indisposition had prompted her to visit her doctor. This being no subject for comment, Judith moved forward, and the two women walked towards the church together.

'Your husband is not with you?' Mrs Coulson asked.

'He is talking to somebody in the inn. I must go back there in ten minutes or so.'

'His inquiries about the poor man Crabtree have brought him to the Jolly Leggers?'

'Well, I think that is what he is discussing now. He is interested in somebody who was staying there last night.'

'I see. I suppose that no stone must be left unturned.'

'Just that.' Judith was amused by this well-worn metaphor. 'All sorts of things can lurk under stones.'

'Yes, indeed. And some of them will be far from pretty.'

Judith was silent. There had been something in Mrs Coulson's voice which she found difficult to know how to respond to.

'I wonder whether it has occurred to Sir John,' Mrs Coulson said, 'that Hollywood may be in danger too?'

'Hollywood – your butler – in danger?' This placid if slightly subterranean lady, Judith was reflecting, could scarcely have uttered more absolutely mysterious words.

'Crabtree came back to Scroop out of the past.' Mrs Coulson had paused at the entrance to the churchyard, and her gaze was travelling slowly over its crumbling evidences of mortality. 'You would agree that the essence of his situation lay in that?'

154

'I suppose it did.'

'He was *bringing* something out of the past. And therefore somebody killed him. I have been thinking about it, Lady Appleby, and that is how it seems to me.'

'I can see it as a possibility. But I don't understand how you relate to it the notion of Hollywood's being in danger.'

'He is the only other person with any direct knowledge of Scroop in Sara Coulson's time.'

'Yes, I see. But Hollywood has been available for killing for a long time. And nobody has killed him yet.'

Mrs Coulson nodded slowly. The gesture might have been an acknowledgement that her line of thought had been not precisely rational. Or it might have been a nod directed, so to speak, to some further inward and unspoken process of her own mind. And she moved forward again towards the church porch.

'As you see,' she said, 'there is a parvis. It is very small – yet hardly smaller than the church itself. The church at Upper Scroop is larger, but I am very fond of this one. You will see a little Saxon work at the east end.'

They walked round the church. Mrs Coulson continued the competent talk of a squire's lady who has done some appropriate home-work in local archaeology. But she had made one very odd remark. And Judith felt a mounting conviction that she was going to make others.

'Shall we go inside?' Mrs Coulson held open a roughly constructed wire door – intended, one supposed, to discourage sheep, cows and others of the brute creation from frequenting the church porch. There were the usual notices and exhortations, including an uncertainly sketched baro- meter or thermometer in red ink, designed to impress upon the faithful how much they yet had to subscribe if the church roof was not to fall down on them.

'Of course, Bertram is responsible for the chancel,' Mrs

Coulson said, studying this. 'The chancel is always the responsibility of the patron of a living. And Bertram doubles any sum subscribed for the upkeep of the rest of the fabric. He is very keen on everything of that sort.'

'He is a strong churchman?'

'I hardly think it can be called that.' The faint irony occasionally to be distinguished in Mrs Coulson's voice was sounding. 'He seems to have no religious convictions. But he always goes to church. And likes to see a good turn-out, as he calls it, of the village people.'

'Yes, I see.' Judith realized, more vividly than before, that the woman beside her harboured rather a large impatience with her husband's conception of his place in society.

They entered the little church and walked round it. There wasn't a great deal upon which to pause until they reached the north transept, which was screened off by some worm-eaten oak.

'This is the tomb,' Mrs Coulson said. 'Don't you like it? The Crabtree Tomb.'

So Judith examined the Crabtree Tomb – thinking, as she did so, that this odd lady had certainly brought off another surprise. Sir William Crabtree lay supine in armour and his wife lay at his side. Beneath them, and in bas-relief, a line of Crabtree sons face a line of Crabtree daughters, all in prayer.

'So the Crabtrees were people of consideration long ago.' Judith turned to Mrs Coulson. 'I felt Seth to be a Thomas Hardy character, but it didn't occur to me that he might be first cousin to Tess. Here's where a kind of fineness in him came from.'

'I'm sure Bertram would think so.' The irony was operative again. 'But I suspect that the Crabtrees have been very simple folk for generations, Lady Appleby. There may be

156

something in blue blood. I don't know. But I doubt whether it can be put in cold storage.'

'So do I. But a clever boy, a sensitive boy, bred in a cottage, may have his whole life conditioned by knowing that his name is on a tomb like this. When he has become aware of it, he may see the gentry with a different eye.'

'And see their wives with a different eye, too.'

Judith had a sudden feeling – perhaps to the credit of her own ancestry – that for the purposes of this sort of conversation it might be seemly to get out of God's blessing and into the warm sun. Mrs Coulson, however, had sat down in a pew.

'I never saw this man Crabtree,' she said. 'You saw him once.'

'Twice. Once living and once dead.'

'And both occasions were only yesterday. I try to think how he must have appeared to you. As an English villager, I suppose, with some overlay of American democratic assurance.'

'Not in the least.' Judith, seeing there was no help for it, sat down in the pew in front of Mrs Coulson, and turned round to speak to her. 'He seemed to me to have taken no colour from his recent years. He was a villager, as you call it, with something else added. I'm not quite sure what. Talent, feeling, sensibility: that was my idea. But I have to admit that my husband felt there was some strain of disingenuousness or concealment in him as well.'

'Something – wicked?' Mrs Coulson hesitated. 'A man who might make unscrupulous use of – well, of something he had stumbled on?'

Judith knew that, for a fraction of a second, she had had hard work not to stare.

'I felt nothing like that,' she said. 'But I'm not sure that he hadn't come back to something he was **very** far from telling us about.'

'Exactly.' Mrs Coulson was eager. 'Something out of the

past. And it must be stopped. That is the important thing.'

'But it *has* been stopped, has it not?' Judith made this point reasonably. 'Somebody has killed Crabtree. Do you think that somebody ought to kill Hollywood as well?'

'There is something mysterious about Hollywood. I discovered that today. It would not surprise me if somebody killed him. I believe somebody will. He knows too much.'

'About the past? Does he know something about the present too?'

'Perhaps. I don't think I greatly mind about the present. Or do I? You see, Lady Appleby, that I am very confused. But I cannot believe that any revelation about the present can hurt anybody that – that I really love. I hope that your husband will discover everything about the present that there is to discover, and that the mystery of Crabtree's death will be sufficiently explained as a result. I hope that we shall not have to have the whole past spread out before us.'

'Mrs Coulson, this seems to me to be a very strange conversation that we are having. I just don't know where to begin trying to make sense of it. About Hollywood, for instance. You say that you discovered something mysterious about him today. What could that have been?'

'The alibi, of course. I am sure your husband didn't believe it. I am sure he saw how surprised I was.'

'If you were surprised, I have no doubt that John detected the fact. But I still don't understand you.'

'Hollywood protected me. He said that I was checking linen with him. It wasn't true.'

'I see. But you didn't say so at the time? You accepted what you call his protection?'

'I had reason to.'

'And he must have known that?'

'He must. He knows a great deal.'

'But why should he do this?'

'I have no idea, Lady Appleby. But I think he is a deep man.'

'Perhaps he is. But there doesn't seem to me to be anything particularly deep in the action of Hollywood's that we are discussing. His protecting you resulted in your protecting him. He knew that you would be grateful for an alibi, and he wanted one himself. That may, or may not, be sinister. In the circumstances, after all, anybody would want an alibi. But there is the fact of the matter. On the terrace of Scroop House, and between the pouring of a glass of Madeira and the handing of a piece of cake, you and your husband's butler cooked up what is undoubtedly a piece of criminal deception between you. I hadn't a notion of it. But you're quite right in supposing it unlikely that it eluded my husband. For anything of the sort, John has pretty well developed a sixth sense. It was rash of you – by which I mean the two of you.'

If this brisk speech surprised Judith as she uttered it, there was no appearance of its correspondingly surprising Mrs Coulson. When the mistress of Scroop House spoke, it was with undiminished composure.

'It was a shock,' she said. 'I mean, my saying nothing. I mean, my not denying Hollywood's story on the instant. But I was silent. Or did I give an actual assent? Perhaps I did. Anyway, my conduct showed me where I had got to. It will scarcely surprise you that I had to go and lie down. And, you see, I was in great fear. Perhaps I am still, although reassurance has been given me. I don't know.'

Judith thought for a moment.

'You felt so – so unwell,' she said, 'that you went to see your doctor? Dr West is your doctor?'

'Dr West is my doctor.' Mrs Coulson raised her chin. She looked straight up the nave of the little church as if confronting whatever the vista thus revealed suggested. 'And he is my lover too.'

'Yes, I see.' Judith had spoken quickly – for she felt that the effect of a shocked silence must definitely not succeed upon what she had just heard. But at least she was puzzled. Mrs Coulson was not terribly bright. But she was a generous sort of woman and nobody could despise her. 'But what I *don't* see is why you haven't gone away with him.'

Mrs Coulson hesitated.

'It has been very recent. A matter of weeks.'

'I still don't see why you haven't gone away with him.'

'It is not possible. It is a matter of his profession. I am Brian's patient at this moment. It would ruin him.'

'Yes, that makes sense, of course. But doesn't that mean – well, a hopeless mess?'

'It does.' This time Mrs Coulson spoke so very composedly that Judith realized she might at any moment abruptly break down. 'Even without – this.'

'This?'

'The old man coming into the boat-house.'

'Mrs Coulson!' Despite her previous speculations, Judith was horrified now. 'Crabtree?'

'Yes. And I simply fled. Through the park. Leaving Brian. It was shameful. I mean the flight. And Brian says he simply hurried away too. But I cannot be quite certain. He is a very passionate man.' Mrs Coulson paused, so that Judith had a grotesque sense that this was something that the unfortunate woman before her would have liked to be more sure of. 'And he was in the power of this horrible intruder.'

'But that is nonsense, surely. You might suppose so, in a mood of panic. But Dr West must be a man of the world, who can quickly assess the limits of such a disaster. He would see that, even if this intruder were unscrupulous and malign, any story he could tell would be a mere unsupported slander.'

'I suppose so.' Mrs Coulson spoke dully now. 'But it is very terrible. And – and disenchanting.'

'Yes.' Judith was silent for a moment, wondering whether there was anything she might venture to say. 'Mrs Coulson, you won't be offended if I tell you how I see this? I see it as some sort of muddle. I think that, if Crabtree hadn't turned up and got killed, it would presently have – well, cleared itself up. Been seen, I mean, as some sort of mistake – as just no go. Not without a great deal of pain, which perhaps you'd have had to share with your husband. I can't say. But something one leaves behind, even if one doesn't forget about. Am I being very impertinent?'

'You are being kind. And truthful. What you say, I know.' Mrs Coulson got this out with a queer dignity. When she spoke again, it was with a slight effect of changing the subject. 'Sometimes I think there is a curse on Scroop House. Or at least on its women. Mrs Binns – and now me.'

'I understand what you mean.' Judith remembered her Uncle Julius's flat statement that Mrs Binns had been an immoral woman; she remembered how – to his subsequent regret – he had hinted that the younger Mrs Coulson had at least the makings of one. And there could be no doubt – she decided – that something of the miserable tragicomedy just recounted had come under his observation during some ramble on the previous afternoon.

'Mrs Binns,' she asked, 'was rather an unsatisfactory person?'

'It is not for me to sit in judgement on her, Lady Appleby. And I never quite understood the matter. When she went away, it was because of some scandal which Bertram must have known of. But he never explained it to me. Whatever it was, Bertram must have judged it a very terrible thing to have happened at Scroop. Because it was certainly the occasion of his asking Mr Binns to leave.'

'In fact, Mrs Coulson, poor Mr Binns lost his house because he had lost his wife?'

'It sounds very absurd. But then, as you have seen, my husband is a little absurd about Scroop. He would like it all to be as in the former Mrs Coulson's time. He keeps everything about the place, you know, precisely as it was then – and, no doubt, he would like me to be a Sara Coulson myself. So anything like a bad kind of life there was something he couldn't bear the thought of. And the result was that out the Binnses went and in we came. I had no say in the matter. Only I did insist that the Binns children should come to us whenever they wanted to.'

'Do you know whether Mrs Binns is still alive?'

'I am almost sure that she is dead. But, you see, nobody ever mentions her.'

'Not even her children in the most casual way?'

'Not even her children. All I have heard is hints dropped among the local people. And, even there, of course, I have never encouraged gossip. What I seem to have gathered is that Mrs Binns had many affairs – but had one particularly disgraceful one of quite long standing. Her husband discovered about it and she vanished. Perhaps she joined the – the guilty party.'

'I see.' The subject didn't seem to Judith one which, in the circumstances, could decently be carried further.

'Of course,' Mrs Coulson said, 'Hollywood must know.'

'Hollywood?' Judith was startled – partly, perhaps, because she was aware of Tarbox's description of his *confrère* at Scroop.

'As I said, Hollywood is like Crabtree. And he has been in a position to know everything. I keep wondering – haven't I said this? – if perhaps he knows something so dangerous that he is in danger himself.'

Chapter Fourteen

Mrs Coulson, it seemed, had a car in the village, and the two women parted at the gate of the churchyard. Judith walked back to the inn. Of what she had learnt in this strange interview, some part was not entirely new – or at least not entirely unsuspected. Of the assignation in the boat-house, and of Crabtree's coming upon it, John had already built up a conjectural picture. Perhaps, too, John had guessed at Dr West as the man involved. And – with equal accuracy, no doubt – John had provided Uncle Julius with his place in the margin of the episode.

That Uncle Julius had himself stepped out of that margin to take an indignant and fatal swipe at Crabtree was plainly absurd. If it was this unfortunate discovery in the boat-house that had led to the old man's death, then it could only be West himself who was the murderer. And West would have a real motive. Mrs Coulson was his patient. If the fact of the liaison got abroad, the result would not be scandal merely but professional ruin as well.

In theory, of course, the murder might have been committed by Mrs Coulson upon the identical motive. The detected lovers appeared to have fled severally and in confusion; neither could be certain of the other's subsequent conduct; each could only reassure the other with protestations of innocence. At least, it must be called a very miserable state of affairs.

Mrs Coulson had said a number of unaccountable things – so many, that Judith felt she ought to count them over in her head now, as an insurance against omitting something important when she presently made a report to John. But when she did run over the conversation in this way, the result was curiously unsatisfactory. She seemed to have taken account of everything, yet there was something she hadn't got round to. Some one thing that Mrs Coulson had said was incompatible with some other thing that Judith positively knew. That was it. Perhaps the point was important, and perhaps it was not. But to grope vainly for it was infuriating. And, in the circumstances, there was only one safe course to adopt. She must try to give John not a synopsis but a verbatim account of the interview. Which meant doing the job at once, while Mrs Coulson's words were fresh in her memory.

But John was not to be found. Nor, for that matter, was Alfred Binns. The little lounge of the Jolly Leggers was deserted. Judith went out again and strolled to the canal. There was nobody in sight on the towpath. John, she decided, must have made some foray of his own into Nether Scroop, and she had missed him. Her best plan was now to wait for him where she was.

She walked towards the tunnel, feeling that its entrance was worth taking another look at. She studied the stonework. She peered inside – but the sun was now in the west and gave no help in distinguishing more than a couple of yards of the interior. She was just about to turn away, when a voice spoke seemingly from the depths of the earth.

'Oh, good. Just take a look round – will you? – for Channing-Kennedy.'

It was John's voice, sounding peculiarly hollow. And it so sounded, of course, because it came from the recesses of the tunnel.

'For pity's sake, John!' Judith took a careful glance around as she spoke. 'No Channing-Kennedy. No sign of anybody.'

'Splendid. Only don't let your modesty be offended. I've

164

left my clothes behind that gate.' In the murk of the tunnel a dimly luminous figure appeared, almost waist-deep in the stagnant water. And it was certainly John. He scrambled blithely to the bank – stark naked, as far as she could see, and very muddy indeed. 'I don't think,' he said, 'that I can get much of it off. But probably it's healthy. It will dry on under my clothes as we walk home. Very similar things are endured in a medicinal way.'

'And just what prompted you to plunge in there?' Judith watched her husband seek the exiguous shelter of a ragged hedge and there begin shaking himself like a spaniel. 'Have you made away with poor Mr Binns, and have you been concealing a body?'

'It wouldn't be a bad place for such a purpose. As a matter of fact, the tunnel is stuffing with bodies. They put them in there to petrify. But perhaps they're very old ones. Leggers, probably. I noticed they had well developed legs.'

'Don't be so idiotic. John. I've just had a most painful interview with that wretched Mrs Coulson, who's been making a frightfully bad job of adultery or near-adultery. And then you must fool like this.'

'Well, well! With that fellow West, I suppose? You can look now. I've put on my trousers.'

'You're quite intolerable. And due for a frightful chill. Don't you know that you're a man in late middle age?'

'Middle middle age. How difficult wet flies are.'

'And now there's a village maiden coming – which serves you right.' Suddenly Judith's voice changed. 'John, it's not a village maiden. It's Daphne Binns. She must know her father's here.'

'But not that we are. We can have a very timely little talk.'

'I had a telephone message,' Daphne Binns said. 'It seems

my father is here.' She frankly stared at Appleby, whose person still bore some evidence of his recent exploit – and who, even in open air, probably smelt of something like ditch-water. 'Have you been diving for more corpses?'

'Something of that sort, Miss Binns. And I've persuaded your father to go for a walk. He's been worrying a good deal. I thought you and I might clear the air a little.'

Daphne wrinkled her nose.

'You might well do that,' she said.

'I'm sorry about that. And I promise to have a good scrubbing before our meeting tonight.'

'Our meeting? I don't know anything about a meeting.'

'There has been no general announcement of it yet. But I somehow think that everybody will be able to attend. It will be at Scroop after dinner. And we shall clear up this unfortunate affair for good. In fact, we shall clear up quite a lot. To my mind, everybody will be the better for it.'

'I don't in the least know what you mean. But I think you are a terribly interfering person.'

Appleby gave a decided nod.

'Yes,' he said. 'That's true. But – this time at least – it's been a matter of fate casting me for the role. I'm the unexpected turn in the story, Miss Binns.'

Judith had climbed up on a gate. It was her favourite rural posture.

'What they call the *deus ex machina*,' she interjected with mild malice. 'Or *ex* whatever the Latin is for a canal.'

Daphne turned towards the tunnel and stared at it.

'Are we going to have a preliminary chat here?' she asked. 'I always disliked this place. I used to dream of having to swim through that tunnel.'

'We can go into the inn, if you like,' Appleby said.

'Go ahead here. I don't mind.' Daphne found a stump and

sat down on it. 'But if everything is going to be cleared up' – she hesitated – 'does that mean that you know who killed the – the old man?'

'No, I don't.'

'Then I can't see –'

'But I can make a good many eliminations. You see, I know *why* he was killed. As you may imagine, that helps a good deal.'

'Well, then – why *was* he killed?' Daphne spoke almost pertly, but Appleby saw that she was trembling.

'It's a perfectly reasonable question, and I'm very sorry that I don't think I should say anything more at the moment, Miss Binns. There are several points that require some thinking about.'

'You seem to have been doing plenty of that.'

'So has everybody else, I imagine. It's almost certain that everybody – everybody who *didn't* kill Crabtree, that is – has by now a pretty fixed notion of who *did*.'

Daphne was startled.

'You mean there's somebody we all suspect?'

'No, I don't. I'd say that each of you, by this time, has his or her own favourite suspect. Yourself, for instance. Haven't you got a suspect?'

'Not all the time. But sometimes – yes. Sometimes I think that *I* must have killed Crabtree.' Daphne Binns had produced this strange statement with a sudden and explosive violence which she must have recognized as odd. For at once she added: 'My God, the ghastly Binnses!'

'Have you dreamt you killed him – as you've dreamt of having to swim through that tunnel?'

'This is a silly conversation, and you're making me say any silly thing that comes into my head.' Daphne was showing signs of the familiar junior Binns' panic. 'I think we should stop it.'

'Before we do that, Miss Binns, what about trying again? Have you an also-ran? If you discovered that you yourself hadn't killed Crabtree, who would be the person you would think of next?'

Daphne Binns produced a cigarette-case and took out a cigarette with an unsteady hand. As an afterthought she offered one to Judith.

'I haven't a clue,' she said.

'Your brother, by any chance?'

'Of course not!' Daphne looked round about her rather desperately. 'Peter is – he's far too damned feeble. I'd say it was – well, I'd say it was Hollywood.'

'That interests me very much. You judge Hollywood to be a sinister character?'

'He's been at Scroop House a long time. He was there when – when Crabtree was there. And I've heard that very bad things were said of him. Perhaps he had committed horrible crimes that Crabtree knew about. So he killed Crabtree as soon as Crabtree came back.'

'Have you any other reason for suspecting Hollywood?'

'No . . . yes.' Daphne had hesitated. 'He told a lie. About where he was when it happened.'

'Certainly he did. But how do you know about it?'

'Oh, damn!' Daphne came out with this admission of incompetence naïvely. 'You'll have to guess, I'm afraid.'

'That isn't terribly difficult. I think that you and Mrs Coulson are a good deal in one another's confidence?'

'Yes.'

'The lie worked two ways, didn't it?'

'Yes. But I won't talk about it.'

'Very well. Let us just take it that Daphne Binns is your first suspect, Hollywood your second – and that your brother doesn't come in at all. By the way, would you say that you and Peter are in one another's confidence?'

'There's not much we don't know about each other, I suppose.'

'You know about Peter and the money?'

'The money?' Daphne's eyes rounded. 'He's owned up?'

'Put it that the facts have owned up for him. Do you think that Crabtree deliberately showed him the hiding-place, or that he discovered it for himself by spying?'

'Crabtree showed it to him. Crabtree was – ' Daphne broke off. 'It's no good my saying anything about Crabtree. I never set eyes on him.'

'Come, come – that is quite inaccurate.' Appleby looked attentively at the confused girl crouched on the stump in front of him. 'You mean that you don't remember much about him, which is quite a different thing. Actually, you have quite strong feelings about him, haven't you? Is that because you know of your father's regarding him as a bad influence on your brother?'

'I haven't any feelings. Except that I'm sure he came back here for some bad reason. He wanted to – to make trouble somehow.'

'Very well. But let us go back to the money. Either because he was thoughtless, or because he was wicked, Crabtree showed Peter some little place of concealment which he had constructed for old Mrs Coulson, and where she had hidden a large sum of money. Peter helped himself to small sums from time to time, and I think this became a kind of guilty secret between him and Crabtree – whom it doesn't, incidentally, exhibit in a very amiable light. An eight- or nine-year-old boy would naturally pilfer from the hoard in a small way, since large sums would be of no use to him. As Peter grew older, he went on pilfering; and as you grew older, you came to know about it. I expect that's right?'

Daphne said nothing, but she nodded slightly.

'Your father ceased being Bertram Coulson's tenant, and

you all left Scroop House, when Peter was about fifteen. It is a five or ten pound note that is useful to a fifteen year-old. But then you and he began coming back on visits. Much of the money was still there, and for Peter the money was the main attraction of a visit to Scroop. Right again?'

'Absolutely right.' Daphne flashed this out. 'And it was meaner, somehow, stealing when a guest here, than it had been when the place seemed to be ours.'

'Perhaps so. But possibly you can answer one question. When Peter was grown up, or felt himself to be grown up, why didn't he take the whole of whatever remained? He could have used it with discreet gradualness.'

'Peter would never do anything in a large way. Small-scale operations are always his line. Didn't I tell you that pinching or slapping the –'

'Yes, but we mustn't go off into irrelevancies.'

'Very well. The largest sum he ever lifted was £300, not terribly long ago, when he badly wanted a better car.'

'Do you think that the news that Crabtree was coming back would put him in a panic?'

'I know it would. I saw it did.' Daphne lifted her chin scornfully. 'And such a little thing!'

'People have come back out of the past to a much graver effect, Miss Binns, I agree.'

'Yes, they have.'

'Would Peter's panic make him desperate?'

'I don't think so. He'd soon begin – well, begin ignoble calculations. That there might be a bit of a row, but that he wouldn't be put in jug. That sort of thing. Peter has rather a worm's mind. I'm afraid I don't sound a very nice kid sister. But I'm quite fond of him, really.'

'I'm not disposed to disbelieve that. Now, may I come back for a moment to Hollywood? We needn't discuss why his lie was convenient to Mrs Coulson. But why was it convenient to him? He may be an innocent man, who followed an ill-judged impulse to make doubly sure he wasn't suspected. Or he may have had some more substantial reason. Mrs Coulson herself seems to think there is something mysterious about him, and even that he may be in the same sort of danger that Crabtree was. Have you any opinion on that?'

'None at all, I'm afraid.'

'You can't see anything that might serve to connect Hollywood and Crabtree?'

'No, I can't. Unless – ' Daphne broke off.

'Yes?'

'They were both womanizers, rather – weren't they?'

'Well, that might be a link.' Appleby spoke absently, as if the conversation had drifted in a direction of no great moment. He took a pace or two towards the canal, looked thoughtfully at the water, and turned back. 'Another thing,' he said. 'Do you think that there is much, or any, of that £2,000 still there?'

'Yes, quite a lot. I suppose old Sara Coulson was a bit of a miser to hide it away. But Peter is really a bit of a miser too. I think he would hate the idea of not having this hoard to go to secretly when he is at Scroop.'

'I see. And he's not afraid that somebody else may find it?' Appleby seemed suddenly struck by another thought. 'By the way, can we be certain that old Sara Coulson didn't establish other hiding places as well? The gossip seems to be that Crabtree, in her last years, made quite a habit of constructing such things for her. If she hid money or valuables once, mightn't she do it several times?'

'I suppose she might. But I don't see – '

'Rightly or wrongly, some people might conclude from the gossip that Scroop is full of such hoards. They might spend years hunting for them. You've never come on anything suspicious in that way? Hollywood, say, crawling around tapping the woodwork?'

Daphne Binns laughed for the first time.

'I'd put nothing beyond him. But I've never seen him on the job. Nor anybody else.'

'And you haven't heard anything, either? It would be a form of exploration carried on stealthily in the night, one imagines. You've never heard strange nocturnal tappings and bumpings and breathings?'

'Well, yes – I have. But it's probably ghosts. Scroop is pretty old.'

Appleby laughed in his turn – for Daphne appeared to have been speaking quite seriously.

'It didn't even terrify you when you were a child?' he asked.

'As a matter of fact, I don't remember anything of the sort then. I'm thinking of much later – just during some of our visits to the Coulsons.'

'I see. Do you think the searcher might be Bertram Coulson himself – searching for the hiding-place not of money but of something else?'

'What a queer idea. It would never have come into my head.'

'No doubt you are right. And you have been very kind, Miss Binns, in discussing the affair with me for so long. I mustn't detain you.'

Daphne stood up.

'Do you know, Sir John, I like you better when you're not making polite speeches? Aren't we rather shying away from things? And are you going to get hold of Peter, and start fishing after me with *him*, as you've been fishing after him with *me*?'

'It is a police technique, I confess. But I see no need to discuss you with your brother.'

'Because you know all the answers already?'

'The relevant ones – yes.'

Daphne Binns had gone pale. Now, suddenly, her colour rose.

'You know the filthy truth?' she said. 'You know that, if I killed Crabtree, it was because I couldn't stick the thought of his presenting himself at Scroop – of his walking into my life – as my father?'

Judith Appleby got off her gate, walked over to Daphne, and shared her stump with her. John, she felt, had managed this turn in the affair rather well. It was much better that Daphne should, in a sense, have come forward with this melancholy piece of family history than that it should have emerged with the effect of being badgered out of her.

'I know,' Appleby was saying quietly, 'that Crabtree may well have been your father. And I know that, whether sensibly or not, the fact was one which you couldn't bear to think of as coming to light. It seemed very large and dreadful to you. And I think it has seemed that, too, to the man whom the law regards as your father today. *That* father – Alfred Binns – has no notion that any inkling of the story has ever come your way.'

'I pieced it together from hints. Or rather Peter and I did.'

'So I have supposed. And the fact will make Mr Binns's task the easier now. When he heard of Crabtree's return, he was perhaps – as he first told me – a little uneasy on Peter's account. But his real anxiety – which he wouldn't disclose to me – was on account of this other thing. He felt that you must be told the truth, and he came down yesterday to do so. He hesitated – and fate stepped strangely in. That is his story.'

'His story, Sir John?'

'For the moment we had better call it that. He has his

story, you have your story, everybody has a story. Tonight, as I have said, we shall get them sorted out. Go on to the inn now. Your father will have returned there.'

'My father?'

'My dear child, it would be folly – and cruel as well – to begin calling him anything else now.'

The Applebys walked back to Pryde in the late afternoon, and Judith described her interview with Mrs Coulson in the church.

'No wonder,' Appleby said, 'that the poor lady was anxious to see Crabtree's death explained in terms of the remote past. She was afraid that West might have done it, simply to protect his professional status.'

'Yes. But in some fantastic corner of her mind she would almost have liked to think that he *had* done it. It would have given him a sort of status as a demon lover that he is a good deal short of measuring up to. As for hoping that Crabtree's death would be explained as resulting from events long ago, I don't think she has been quite whole-hearted. They might somehow touch her husband rather nearly – and I imagine she is very fond of him still. Again, she is clearly fond of Daphne. And it may well be that she knows the child's secret.' Judith paused. 'By the way, how did *you* tumble to it?'

'As so often, the truth just built itself up. When we first saw Peter and Daphne, I recognized Alfred Binns in Peter at once. Daphne, on the other hand, puzzled me. I had a vague feeling that I had seen her before, and the fact stuck in my head. Then again, when the two children were savaging each other, Daphne said that Crabtree had "shown Peter all sorts of things", and Peter presently retorted that Crabtree "had got in a lot of places where he shouldn't". He was plainly saying something not very nice, and again the thing stuck in my head. But the point at which the truth became inescapable was when I learnt that Alfred Binns had actually paid Crabtree – Crabtree, who had been a great one with the ladies – a substantial sum of money to depart overseas. When I made it clear to Binns that the outline of the affair wasn't mysterious to me, he told me the final truth of the matter. When Mrs Binns eventually vanished, it was for the purpose of joining her former lover Crabtree in America. But she died soon after.'

'And do you think that Crabtree's return was really for the purpose of making capital out of being Daphne's father?'

'Perhaps it was. Perhaps he merely had a natural desire to see the child and be in some sense acknowledged; or perhaps what was chiefly in his mind was something totally different. Two things were evident at our encounter with him. He did have some position or intention that he wasn't concerned should appear. And something had puzzled or disconcerted him.'

'At least he contrived to do a good deal of disconcerting himself. His coming upon Mrs Coulson and Dr West was pure chance. But almost everybody else in the affair appears to have been badly bothered by him in what might be called a meaningful way.'

'Quite so. But the question is: which of them was brought to the pitch of murder, and why? If everybody is to have a favourite suspect, who is yours?'

'Oh, Alfred Binns.' Having convinced herself that John was now as near possessing the solution of the mystery as made no matter, Judith spoke without much feeling of responsibility. 'Daphne is really more than a daughter to him, not less. He believed Daphne to be ignorant of the truth, and he believed that she would find it shattering. He was prepared to do anything rather than have it raked up.'

'It's a tenable theory. Of course, Daphne *was* shattered;

so shattered, despite her previous knowledge, that one can imagine her doing almost anything. To be publicly viewed as the offspring not merely of an adulterous relationship, but of an adulterous relationship with a servant: that was the unbearable thing. The poor child possesses no sort of background or education to stand up to it.'

'She might take some comfort from the Crabtree Tomb. There were Crabtrees centuries before there were Binnses. And the peasant Seth Crabtree, for that matter, had a certain fineness not to be distinguished in the bourgeois Alfred Binns.' Judith was silent for a moment. 'But my speculations on the case are over,' she said. 'I don't know where to begin, and I think you do.'

'Yes, I know where to begin. With the barge.'

'The barge, John?' Judith was entirely at a loss.

'The beautifully carved little barge which Crabtree made long ago.'

'*That* is important?'

'Its disappearance from beside Crabtree's body is.'

Judith thought for a moment.

'It contained a missing will – something like that?'

'Nothing so melodramatic. It might simply have reminded somebody of a significant and awkward fact.'

Chapter Fifteen

The company gathered in the library of Scroop House was a large one. There was a corresponding largeness about the tray with glasses and decanters which was being brought in by a parlourmaid. And Bertram Coulson, although he wore a preoccupied air, turned to her disapprovingly.

'These things are too heavy for you, Jane. You ought not to be single-handed. Where is Hollywood?'

Jane looked disconcerted.

'If you please, sir, Mr Hollywood is nowhere to be found. And Mrs Roberts said I had better bring the things myself.'

'Then Mrs Roberts was quite right. But surely it isn't Hollywood's evening off?'

'No, sir. But nobody can find him.'

The parlourmaid fled. Bertram Coulson turned back to his guests with an air of having to apologize for having thus aired a purely domestic matter.

'Sir John is in charge,' he said. 'And I see no need for any preliminaries. We are all known to each other. Except, possibly, this gentleman.' And Coulson turned rather dubiously towards the innkeeper from the Three Leggers.

'David Channing-Kennedy, sir' Mr Channing-Kennedy had thought it proper to put on a purple velvet smoking jacket of Edwardian suggestion to visit Scroop, and he was thus in a much grander turn-out than anybody else. 'Herefordshire Channing-Kennedys, as a matter of fact. And, of course, the jolly old R.A.F. Run the pub at Nether Scroop now, as a matter of fact. Never brought you along some letters of introduction. But delighted to drop in in this informal way.' Mr Channing-Kennedy smiled affably behind his enormous moustache. But his eyes were not those of a man in whom delight is in fact a predominant emotion.

'Very pleased to have you,' Bertram Coulson said a shade stiffly. 'But we mustn't pretend that this is a social occasion. Sir John Appleby is in charge, as I have said. Sir John.'

Thus formally charged, Appleby stood up.

'We are met,' he said, 'to clear up Seth Crabtree's death. Perhaps some explanation is needed of my asking one or two people to come along. Mr Channing-Kennedy, as he has just mentioned, manages the Jolly Leggers, in which Crabtree spent some of his last hours. Dr West' – Appleby paused for a fraction of a second – 'happened to have a certain stretch of the canal under his observation during part of yesterday afternoon. So, as it happened, did Colonel Raven, who – '

'Who saw nothing at all.' It was the Colonel himself who had thus firmly interrupted. 'I have felt it as my duty to come along, as a neighbourly act to Coulson' – the Colonel's tone became yet firmer – 'and Mrs Coulson. But I saw nothing at all.'

'And moreover,' Appleby went on smoothly, 'Colonel Raven's memories of this part of the country extend a fairly long way back. So he may be useful to us. These, I think, are the only preliminary remarks needed. We can now clear the matter up.'

'What do you mean by clearing the matter up?' It was Dr West who spoke. 'Simply discovering who killed this old man?'

'Just that, sir. Who killed him, and why. We have no other topic of inquiry before us. I think it is a fact, Dr West, that you saw Crabtree yesterday afternoon?'

'Certainly. It must have been a little before half past one.

He appeared to have crossed the canal by the lock, and to be taking a look at the old boat-house.'

'He went inside?'

'I think not. I believe it is commonly kept locked. But I cannot be certain, since I was merely walking past.'

'Thank you. Mrs Coulson, I believe it so happens that you can confirm this?'

'Yes, Sir John. I had taken a walk through the park, and I did just glimpse somebody who was probably Crabtree.'

'Am I right in thinking that this doesn't quite square with something your butler said earlier today?'

'Yes, indeed. Hollywood described us as engaged together in examining the table linen. But in fact he was thinking of the day before, and I failed to notice the confusion.'

'Quite so.' Appleby nodded calmly. 'Such confusions may, of course, be unfortunate when related to criminal occurrences. But it is unlikely that this one need bother us again. We now have Crabtree observed close to the lock – and alive not very long before his body was discovered in it. We have to deal with only a short span of time. And now let us consider the matter more at large.' Appleby looked round with the appearance of a kind of innocent vagueness. 'Why should anybody want to kill him?'

'Wasn't he coming back to this place after a great many years – and proposing to tell tales about happy times gone by?'

It was Channing-Kennedy who offered this suggestion – smiling agreeably round the company as he did so.

'That is a most interesting suggestion.' Appleby seemed much struck by the novelty of the idea Channing-Kennedy had produced. 'But tales about whom? We might go round this gathering and try to discover. And we might begin almost at random. Say, with Mr Peter Binns.'

'With me?' Peter Binns, who had been staring gloomily round the room, sat up with a jerk.

'Yes, Mr Binns. Would you say that Crabtree had a tale to tell about you?'

'Yes, I suppose so.' Rather surprisingly, Peter spoke straight out.

'To your discredit – which I take to be Mr Channing-Kennedy's general idea?'

'Yes, to my discredit, all right.'

'Grave discredit?'

'I don't think I'd call it that. It began when I was a kid, and – and went on for a bit. Something about money. Not terribly nice, I'm afraid.'

'But not something that would have prompted you to smash in this old man's head?'

There was a startled silence.

'Oh, no,' Peter Binns said simply. 'It wouldn't be my sort of thing.'

'That seems a reasonable point.' Appleby nodded, not unkindly, at the young man. 'So let us next consider your sister. In the context, I mean, of Crabtree's telling tales. Miss Binns, could Crabtree have said or revealed anything at all which could in any way reflect discredit on anything you ever did?'

'No, he couldn't.' Daphne Binns had taken a deep breath by way of response to the dexterity of Appleby's question.

'Thank you.' Appleby turned to Alfred Binns. 'Mr Binns, I think the matter is rather different in your case?'

'I agree.'

'You had once been uneasy about Crabtree's influence over your son?'

'Yes.'

'But not to an immoderate or irrational degree?'

'I think not.'

'You know now, I think, that Crabtree had been blame-worthy in putting a certain temptation to dishonesty in Peter's way when he was quite small?'

'I do.'

'It is a subject which we can dismiss, I think – although, of course, it was your uneasiness from long ago that brought you down here yesterday. So far, then, we don't appear to be making a great deal of progress – except in rather a negative way. And it now seems as if our host is the only person whom it remains to question in regard to Mr Chan-ning-Kennedy's conjecture. Mr Coulson, I think I am right in supposing that you set eyes on Crabtree for the first time in your life not much more than a couple of hours before his death?'

'That is so.'

'So there doesn't seem much possibility that Crabtree had returned bringing trouble for you?'

'That doesn't follow, I'm afraid.' Bertram Coulson had shaken his head decidedly. 'No – that doesn't follow at all.'

'Crabtree's turning up as he did,' Bertram Coulson went on, 'made me very uneasy. He was civil, but I had an obscure sense that he had some unconfessed aim. This might have had nothing to do with me. But I was alarmed. In giving an account of my meeting with him yesterday, I have to confess that I was not frank about that. What is in question is the validity of my title to Scroop.'

'Would it surprise you to learn,' Appleby asked, 'that Crabtree got drunk in Mr Channing-Kennedy's inn the evening before he came to see you, and swore that he could have you turned out of Scroop if he wanted to? Mr Channing-Kennedy, that is more or less what you reported to me?'

'Quite right.' Channing-Kennedy did not speak without a shade of hesitation. 'Sorry to say anything that may be upsetting. But that was the kind of talk this old rascal was putting up.'

'That surprises you?' Appleby repeated, turning to Coulson.

'Well, yes – it does. Not that I quite know why. For I have always, you see, had a slight uneasiness about being here. There was another Coulson you may have heard of – Miles Coulson – who was commonly expected to be Sara Coulson's heir and successor. What has always been in my head is something like this. At a certain point the old lady left the place to me. Later, and when entirely in her right mind, she made a will leaving it to Miles. But right at the end, and when decidedly eccentric, she hid it away where it has never been found. Something like that. Now Crabtree was in some obscure way in her confidence, and it was not improbable that he would know where this instrument was concealed. So his appearing at Scroop stirred up an old anxiety in my mind.'

'What utter nonsense!' It was Alfred Binns who spoke impatiently. 'A little knowledge of the law – '

'That is what my husband said.' Judith interrupted in her turn. 'But I wanted to point out to him that the law wasn't the point. Mr Coulson has a very high sense of responsibility about Scroop. He would feel absolutely bound to honour a wish of old Mrs Coulson's, even if it were found to have no legal force.'

Dr West suddenly leant forward in his chair.

'Isn't this very great nonsense?' he asked acidly. 'If Mr Coulson is the sort of person who has these delicate feelings about the ownership of his estate, then he certainly didn't kill Crabtree on the off-chance that Crabtree was bringing him trouble in the matter. It seems to me that this inquiry is getting nowhere. We may still be sitting here at midnight.'

'Midnight is my dead-line, as a matter of fact,' Appleby

said easily. 'But I hope we shall all be asleep by then. Or nearly all of us.'

'Glad to hear it,' Channing-Kennedy said heartily. 'Brandy and shut-eye will be just right by me. Can't help feeling all this is rather a lot of fuss about an old peasant. Hope I don't speak out of turn.' He looked round affably. 'Anybody care for a drop of anything now?'

This odd importation of Mr Channing-Kennedy's professional character into the library of Scroop House appeared mildly to surprise Bertram Coulson. He fetched Channing-Kennedy a drink, looking at him a little wonderingly as he did so.

'For goodness' sake,' Daphne Binns said suddenly, '*let's get on.*'

'Then may I make a fresh start?' Appleby looked round to gather the attention of the company. 'I want to forget about a hypothetical missing will, and consider something else that I myself know to be missing. I mean a small carved model of a canal barge, the work of Seth Crabtree when he was quite a young man. Mr Channing-Kennedy ought to know what I mean, for the thing apparently stood on a chimney-piece in his inn for a great number of years.'

'I think I've noticed what you mean.' Channing-Kennedy sounded puzzled and uneasy. 'But I've never had the thing in my hands. Only been here a few years, you know. Herefordshire's my part.'

'Crabtree took it with him when he left your inn yesterday. It was his property, and he presumably felt entitled to do so. But when his body was found, the little barge had disappeared. Careful search has failed to bring it to light. So the only possible conclusion is that the murderer took it away with him.'

There was a baffled silence.

'It couldn't be valuable?' Peter Binns asked.

'I think not. Still, it was very beautifully made. And that is the point.' Appleby stood up and turned to Bertram Coulson. 'I wonder whether I might have your leave for Hilliard's people to bring in an exhibit?'

'An exhibit?' Coulson was startled. 'Anything you like.'

Amid another baffled silence Appleby crossed the library and threw open the beautiful double doors which were its main entrance. He stood back, and there was a sound of heavy movement outside. Then four constables entered. They were carrying with effort a large oblong wooden crate. They lowered it carefully to the floor and withdrew.

'How did you come by that?' Channing-Kennedy asked the question.

'From close by the Jolly Leggers, as a matter of fact. It was on a punt, some twenty yards inside the tunnel.'

'How damned odd.' Channing-Kennedy drained his glass and stood up. He gave Bertram Coulson his affable smile. 'Have another of these, old boy, if you don't mind.' He strolled over to the table with the decanters, which stood in a window embrasure. 'And what's inside?'

'Inside the crate?' Appleby paused. 'Do you know Mr Coulson's butler?'

'Of course I don't know Mr Coulson's butler.'

'I thought you might. His name's Hollywood. And what is inside the crate is Hollywood's dead body.'

This time, the silence was a stunned one. It was broken by Mrs Coulson, who gave a low cry.

'In a manner of speaking, that is to say.' Appleby looked straight at Channing-Kennedy. 'Put it that what is in that crate means that Hollywood is as good as a dead man. Or say a hanged man. Quite prosaically, what the crate contains is something – or something looking like – what would be

184

called a Chinoiserie decorated Chinese lacquer kneehole writing table of Serpentine shape.'

These fantastic words had an instantaneous and equally fantastic sequel. There was a crash of glass, and Channing-Kennedy disappeared into the night.

Outside, the engine of a car burst into life, whistles blew, there was some shouting. Appleby turned back into the library. His racing and chasing days were over; all that was somebody else's job.

'Exit Channing-Kennedy,' he said. 'If he comes back, it won't be as Channing-Kennedy. It will be as Miles Coulson.'

'I knew it.' Bertram Coulson had stood up. 'When he offered my brandy round, I knew in my heart that it was he.'

Chapter Sixteen

'May I go back a little?' Appleby asked. The uproar of flight and pursuit had faded into the night. 'The little barge was beautifully made. And that was the point. Seth Crabtree was an admirable carpenter, well able to make clever little hiding-places for Mrs Coulson in her last years. But he was more. He was a superb natural craftsman. *When her choicest pieces needed repair, Crabtree did the job.* He was the Grand Collector's right-hand man. And remember that Sara Coulson *was* the Grand Collector.'

'Ormolu and O.M.s,' Colonel Raven said. 'Pottery and prima donnas.'

'Precisely. And two things stick out about Scroop House, all through the record. Sara Coulson filled it with the very finest things from cellars to attics. And all this has been preserved *in situ.* The house was let furnished immediately she died. Later, Mr Bertram Coulson took over, and kept everything as it was. Just as – well, just as an antique shop, the place was a treasure-house of the first order. Crudely put, the furniture was worth a fortune.'

'And so it is,' Bertram Coulson said. 'I have the valuation for probate. And I've been told that the market value of the stuff has increased fantastically since then.'

'Quite so. A few weeks ago, a Louis XV black and gold lacquer commode fetched $48,000 in New York. Do you mind, Coulson, if I have in those Bobbies again?'

The constables returned. They lifted the lid of the crate. Regardless of litter, they removed a good deal of wood-wool. And then they produced a piece of furniture.

'Would you be so very kind' – Appleby said, with the unconscious extreme courtesy of a remote superior: so that Judith was amused – 'as to take it down there, and put it beside the other one?'

The constables did as they were told. Appleby nodded to them. They went away. And the company stared, stupefied.

'This has been a connoisseur's case,' Appleby said. 'Or, rather, two connoisseurs. Crabtree being the one, and my wife being the other. Crabtree had just one glimpse of the hall and staircase here. And he was a disconcerted and puzzled man. The fine things – which had chiefly drawn him back to Scroop – seemed not *quite* the same. Hollywood knew that, if this disastrously returned *émigré* had one further straight look at the furniture, the game would be up. That is why he followed him to the Jolly Leggers, spied on him there, dogged him to the lock, and killed him. *It's why he took away the little barge.* It must come back into nobody's head that Crabtree had been the craftsman he was. Do I make myself clear?'

Bertram Coulson was staring at the two identical writing tables, now standing side by side.

'No,' he said. 'I can make nothing of it, at all.'

'This morning, you showed Judith over Scroop. When I asked her about it, she reported that it contained some superb pieces, and a great deal of "ultra shiny high-grade reproduction antique". You mustn't be offended by this. It's important.'

'My dear man, of course I'm not offended. Do you take me for a furniture dealer?' Bertram Coulson spoke briskly and without self-consciousness – so that Appleby had an impression that he had listened, almost for the first time, to one who was the natural master of Scroop.

'Later today, Mrs Coulson reiterated to my wife how you

had a passion for keeping everything about the place precisely as it was in Sara Coulson's time. And my wife had an obscure sense that she had been told something that simply didn't match with something else. That something else was, in fact, all the nicely made replicas – the "high-grade reproduction antique" – which Miles Coulson, alias Channing-Kennedy, and Hollywood have been substituting over a number of years for the real thing.'

'It doesn't make sense.' Alfred Binns spoke up violently. 'It simply doesn't make economic sense.'

'I assure you that it does. Marketing stolen Old Masters and so forth is very difficult. Marketing stolen antique furniture, however superb, is dead easy. And fantastically profitable. Just you try to buy, in London or Rome or New York, a gentleman's social table by Hepplewhite.'

'Or a Gothic cabinet by Chippendale,' Judith said. 'Or a Louis XVI semainier, or a French provincial commode before about 1750, or a set of quartetto tables, or a Grecian squab, or a couple of Herculaneums, or some girandoles by Matthias Lock, or even a garden seat by William Halfpenny –'

'My wife studies these things,' Appleby interrupted rather hastily. 'And you see the situation. It paid these people – your distant cousin Miles and the rascal Hollywood – many times over to have exact replicas made, and to substitute them, piece by piece, for the real thing. You yourself, you know' – and Appleby glanced disarmingly at Bertram Coulson – 'have never made a study of these things. Mrs Coulson is not one with any particular eye for the mere inanimate paraphernalia of living. And your guests – as Colonel Raven put it to me in a slightly different form of words – are not collectors and aesthetes and people of that sort. Miles Coulson – the dispossessed Miles Coulson, as he felt himself to be – was an actor, you remember, and had no difficulty in turning innkeeper. He enjoyed the Apart.

gentleman, pretending to be a vulgarian pretending to be a gentleman: it was great fun.'

Appleby paused and glanced at his watch – perhaps with a shade of anxiety.

'I don't know whether,' he said, 'you'll want me, just at this hour, to dot all the *I*'s and cross all the *t*'s. But consider your disused canal, and that mysterious tunnel. It would be hard to manage even a nocturnal traffic unobserved by way of Upper Scroop. The village presses hard upon the house. But the canal, the old boat-house and the tunnel were absolutely ideal for the job. By the way, you were never aware of any mysterious bumpings in the night?'

'Never.' Bertram Coulson passed a hand over his forehead in a dazed gesture.

'Miss Binns was. But she decided it was a matter of ghosts and so of no importance.'

Everybody was silent. And, into the silence, broke the shrill summons of a telephone bell.

'It will be for me, I think.' Appleby turned to Bertram Coulson. 'Do you mind?' He went over to the instrument and picked it up. 'Yes,' he said, 'Appleby.' Then he listened in silence – in a silence that seemed unnaturally long. 'Thank you,' he said quietly, and hung up.

'They've been – been caught?' Daphne Binns asked timidly.

'Not precisely that.' Appleby glanced first at Judith and then at the rest of the company. 'Hollywood had made himself scarce with the idea of having a car ready if the game should really prove to be up. I was in favour of giving him some play. Flight would be good evidence. That is entirely my responsibility, and not Hilliard's.'

'You mean they've got away?' Peter Binns demanded.

'Not that either. They got out of the park, and clear on the

189

high road. But Hilliard was on top of them. They got to your county town. And there they crashed.'

'Crashed?' Colonel Raven said sharply.

'Yes. Straight through a plate glass window and half across the shop that lay behind it. They're both dead.'

There was silence. And faintly from the stables of Scroop House, a clock was heard to chime.

'Midnight?' Judith asked.

Appleby shook his head.

'Eleven,' he said. 'I thought we'd have a margin.' He smiled – and then looked seriously about him. 'By the way,' he said. 'The shop. It was a furniture shop. And there's nothing to do but disperse and go to bed.'

More About Penguins

If you have enjoyed reading this book you may wish to
know that *Penguin Book News* appears every month. It is an
attractively illustrated magazine containing a complete list
of books published by Penguins and still in print, together
with details of the month's new books. A specimen copy
will be sent free on request.

Penguin Book News is obtainable from most bookshops;
but you may prefer to become a regular subscriber at
3s. for twelve issues. Just write to Dept EP, Penguin Books
Ltd, Harmondsworth, Middlesex, enclosing a cheque or
postal order, and you will be put on the mailing list.

Other Penguins by Michael Innes are listed on the
following page.

Note: *Penguin Book News* is not available in the U.S.A.

Michael Innes

'Mr Innes can write any other detective novelist out of sight. His books will stand reading again and again' – *Time and Tide*

'The most able writer of grotesque fantasy in crime fiction' – *Birmingham Post*

'Mr Innes engages the fourteen-year-old in high-brows' – T. C. Worsley on the B.B.C.

'A master – he constucts a plot that twists and turns like an electric eel: it gives you shock upon shock and you cannot let go' – *The Times Literary Supplement*

The following Penguins by Michael Innes are available

The Daffodil Affair
Death at the President's Lodging
Hamlet, Revenge!
Hare Sitting Up
The Journeying Boy
Old Hall, New Hall
Operation Pax
Silence Observed
Weight of the Evidence

Not for sale in the U.S.A.